"I'm hanging out with Conner later," Tia said. "He just broke up with Alanna, and our normally stoic friend is kind of a basket case."

Elizabeth's heart took an unexpected lurch. She couldn't believe Conner and Alanna had broken up. She'd thought everything was great between them. Not that she knew firsthand. She and Conner hadn't spoken to each other in weeks. But whenever her friends talked about the couple, it was like they were discussing Romeo and Juliet. Without the tragic ending.

"I probably shouldn't be telling you this," Tia continued. "I mean . . . I'm sure you don't want to discuss Conner's love life."

"No! No. It's okay," Elizabeth said, hoping the blush in her cheeks would come off as redness from the exertion of gym class. Why was the fact that Conner was single getting to her so much? She'd buried that relationship a long time ago. A *long* time ago.

"But you're with Jeff now anyway, so I don't know why I thought this news would, you know, affect you," Tia said.

"It doesn't," Elizabeth replied with a shake of her head. "Not at all."

There was no reason for her to care that Conner and Alanna had broken up. So why did she? It was probably just that this was the first time since *she'd* broken up with Conner that he was single and she had a boyfriend. It felt kind of nice, in a weird way.

But like Tia said, she was with Jeff now. And she was happy that way.

Don't miss any of the books in SWEET VALLEY HIGH
SENIOR YEAR, an exciting series from Bantam Books!

Visit the Official Sweet Valley Web Site on the Internet at:

www.sweetvalley.com

Francine Pascal's SVH senioryear

He's Back

CREATED BY
FRANCINE PASCAL

BANTAM BOOKS
NEW YORK • TORONTO • LONDON • SYDNEY • AUCKLAND

RL: 6, AGES 012 AND UP

HE'S BACK
A Bantam Book / May 2002

Sweet Valley High® is a registered trademark of Francine Pascal.
Conceived by Francine Pascal.
Cover photography by Michael Segal.

Produced by 17th Street Productions,
an Alloy, Inc. company.
151 West 26th Street
New York, NY 10011.

ISBN: 0-553-49390-6

Visit us on the Web! www.randomhouse.com/teens

Published simultaneously in the United States and Canada

Bantam Books is an imprint of Random House Children's Books, a
division of Random House, Inc. BANTAM BOOKS and the rooster
colophon are registered trademarks of Random House, Inc. Bantam Books,
1540 Broadway, New York, New York 10036.

PRINTED IN THE UNITED STATES OF AMERICA

OPM   0 9 8 7 6 5 4 3 2 1

To Hilary Tate Peckos

Elizabeth Wakefield

Ex-boyfriends, ex-friends, ex-relationships of all kinds are weird things. When you first break up with somebody, you're totally and completely sure you're never going to speak to them again. Never going to look at them again. The thought of even being in the same room with that person seems totally unfathomable. Even if it's not an angry breakup, you just can't imagine ever feeling comfortable being casual with someone after all that time of being so close.

I think that's why it took Todd and me such a long time to become friends again. Okay, we're not exactly <u>friends</u> right now, but I can imagine a day when we will be. When we'll actually be able to hang out with each other without constantly tripping all over ourselves.

And then there's Jeff. I hadn't talked to him in forever, and now he's back in my life and it's better than it ever was.

There are some relationships, however, that cannot be returned to. Some relationships that are better left dead and buried. Buried deep, deep, <u>deep</u> below the ground.

Conner McDermott

I've been out with a lot of girls. A lot of girls. And I can honestly say I'm not friends with a single one of them today. Not one.

I'm not saying that it can't happen. I've just never seen it work out.

Alanna Feldman

You can be friends with an ex. It's the mature thing to do, actually. The mature way to live your life.

Of course if the ex has stabbed you in the back with an especially sharp knife and twisted it a few times, that could pose a bit of a problem, don't you think?

melissa Fox

Will's the only person I've ever dated, and he's never been my ex long enough to find out whether or not we can be friends. I don't see it working, though. I mean, I could be civil to him, but I don't think Will could handle it. There's just too much history there. Too much resentment. Too much negative energy.

Yes, Will and I have broken up and gotten back together too many times to count. But I have a feeling that trend is going to end very soon. And for good.

Jeremy Aames

Friends with an ex, huh? Well, Jessica is my first real girlfriend. And when we broke up, well, let's just say I didn't exactly find it easy to be around her. It was kind of painful, actually. Kind of leg-broken-in-three-places painful.

But I'd like to think I could be a big enough man to be friends with an ex eventually. You know, after the wounds healed or whatever. Still, I know myself well enough to know that it would have to depend on the nature of the breakup. If it was a huge betrayal—if someone had done something really awful to me—I doubt I could ever be friends with that person again.

I've never been all that good at forgiving and forgetting. Not when something big is at stake. Call it a character flaw. Everyone has to have at least one, right?

CHAPTER 1
Romeo and Juliet—Without the Tragic Ending

"I *hate* sit-ups!" Tia Ramirez groaned as she pulled herself up off the mat in gym class and touched her elbows to her knees. "I hate *crunches*, I hate *sit-ups*, I don't need abs of steel."

"Right. You already *have* abs of steel," Elizabeth Wakefield answered, pushing a sweaty strand of blond hair away from her face. She pressed harder into Tia's feet to hold them down as her friend struggled to sit up again. "Look at you. You could pose for the cover of *Muscle & Fitness*."

"Whatever," Tia said, rolling her big brown eyes. "You have a flat stomach too."

"Flat, maybe. Strong, nuh-uh," Elizabeth said. She glanced across the gym at the sadistic instructor, Coach Riley, and mentally willed him to blow the whistle. She'd had just about enough of gym class for one day, thank you very much. Her stomach was still killing from her own fifty sit-ups, and she desperately needed to wash her face before returning to class.

1

"How many have I done?" Tia whispered, leaning on her knees to take a breather.

Elizabeth scrunched up her brow. "Um . . . fifty?" she said.

"I love you!" Tia responded, giving Elizabeth a big air kiss. She pulled her long brown hair out of her ponytail and lay back on the mat, fanning her hair out around her like a huge mane.

"Good! Then you and Trent will go out with me and Jeff tonight," Elizabeth said with a grin. She let go of Tia's feet and flopped back next to her friend. "I mean, if you love me so much."

Tia was silent for a bit too long. Especially since the question wasn't exactly a mind bender. Elizabeth turned to look at her.

"I . . . can't tonight," Tia said, fiddling with the drawstring on her heather gray sweatpants. "Trent and I weren't exactly planning on getting together, and . . ."

Tia's sentence trailed off, and she didn't elaborate.

"Oookay," Elizabeth said after waiting a few seconds for the hanging sentence to be finished. She rolled over onto her stomach and propped herself up on her elbows. "What's going on?" she asked.

"Nothing," Tia said.

"Whatever. You're obviously forgetting two important points here," Elizabeth said, holding up two fingers. "One, you suck at lying, and two, I'm now a professional journalist. I know a story when I see one."

"All right, all right, your powers are far too strong for me," Tia said sarcastically.

She looked at Elizabeth again, her eyes concerned, like she was gauging Elizabeth's mood before she said whatever it was she was going to say. Elizabeth felt her pulse quicken. What was going on?

"I'm hanging out with Conner this afternoon," Tia explained finally, wrapping the string around her finger. "He just broke up with Alanna, and our normally stoic friend is kind of a basket case."

Elizabeth's heart took an unexpected lurch, and she knew it was reflected in her face. She blinked and looked away, trying to hide it. She couldn't believe Conner and Alanna had broken up. She'd thought everything was great between them. Not that she knew firsthand. She and Conner hadn't spoken to each other in weeks. But whenever her friends talked about the couple, it was like they were discussing Romeo and Juliet. Without the tragic ending.

"I probably shouldn't be telling you this," Tia said, bringing her hands to her face as Elizabeth squirmed up into a sitting position. "I mean . . . I'm sure you don't want to discuss Conner's love life."

"No! No. It's okay," Elizabeth said, hoping the blush in her cheeks would come off as redness from the exertion of gym class. Why was the fact that Conner was

3

single getting to her so much? She'd buried that relationship a long time ago. A *long* time ago.

"I just figured I might as well tell you," Tia explained. She sat up and tilted her head to look at Elizabeth, squinting one eye. "You were going to find out anyway. And I just wanted you to know why I might be spending more time with Conner."

"Of course. That's totally cool," Elizabeth said.

"And you're with Jeff now anyway, so I don't know why I thought this news would, you know, affect you," Tia said.

"It doesn't," Elizabeth replied with a shake of her head. "Not at all."

"Good," Tia said, standing and wiping her sweaty hands on her thighs. "'Cause Jeff is on his way over here right now."

Elizabeth's heart jumped nervously as Tia quickly walked away, joining a couple of her friends from the cheerleading squad on the other side of the room. Elizabeth took a deep breath. There was nothing to be nervous about. What was wrong with her? She glanced over her shoulder and saw Jeff striding over to her, a killer grin on his face.

"Hey, beautiful," he said, dropping onto the floor next to her. Elizabeth grinned at his greeting and leaned forward for a quick kiss.

"Hey, yourself," she said. "Did you do all your sit-ups?"

"Sure did," Jeff said, lifting his shirt to expose his rock-hard stomach, perfected from hours of snowboarding and surfing. He slapped his stomach once and looked at her. "Not bad, huh?"

Elizabeth blushed again, but at least this time it was for the right guy. "Not at all," she said as Coach Riley finally blew the whistle, ending class.

Jeff rose to his feet and pulled Elizabeth up. "So, are we going out with Tia and Trent tonight?" he asked as they made their way to the locker rooms.

"No, not tonight," Elizabeth said, looking at the floor and hoping he didn't ask for more of an explanation. Luckily Jeff moved on to the subject of where to eat and which movie to see. As he weighed the pros and cons of Italian versus Mexican, Elizabeth focused on breathing regularly and putting Conner out of her mind. There was no reason for her to care that he and Alanna had broken up. It was probably just that this was the first time since *she'd* broken up with Conner that he was single and she had a boyfriend. It felt kind of nice, in a weird way.

She reached over and grabbed Jeff's hand, lacing her fingers through his. Yep. She was with Jeff now. And she was happy that way.

Don't do it, man. Just don't do it.

Conner McDermott stared at the cordless phone

lying on the corner of his desk. His hands were itching to pick it up, but he couldn't let himself. He could not go there. He could not allow himself to be that pathetic.

"You know if you call, you're just going to get her machine," he told himself. He spun his desk chair around and picked up the *Rolling Stone* magazine from the foot of his bed, flipping through the well-worn pages. But even as he did, his head started to turn again, gradually moving his body with it, until he was facing the phone again.

"Dammit," he said under his breath. He grabbed the phone, picked it up, and dialed quickly with his thumb.

She's not going to pick up, the little voice in his head teased him as his jaw clenched. One ring. Two rings.

"Come on . . . come on. . . ."

Three rings. Four . . .

"Hi! This is Alanna! I'm not here right—"

Conner clicked off the phone and tossed it on his bed, where it bounced once, hit the wall, and then ricocheted off and crashed to the floor. He had no idea why he kept doing this to himself. Ever since Alanna had gotten back from Chicago, she'd refused to pick up the phone. He'd known she was going to be mad at him, but what was she going to do, ignore him forever?

That's probably what you'd do, his brain reminded him.

Conner hung his head. He wasn't the most forgiving guy in the world. And he knew that if he'd run off to another state and Alanna had brought his mother to find him, he'd probably be giving the silent treatment forever.

Taking a deep breath, Conner pushed himself out of his chair and lay down on his bed, staring up at the ceiling. He couldn't believe this was what he had come to—spending Saturday afternoon brooding. But then, he'd never felt quite like this before—like someone kept pulling his heart out and mashing it with a meat grinder every single day.

"All right, that's it," Conner said to himself, sitting up again and planting his feet on the floor. If she didn't want to recognize the fact that he was just trying to help her, that was her problem. And if she never wanted to talk to him again, well, then that was her loss.

Conner got up and grabbed his guitar off the stand in the corner. He was about to sit down and get to work on a new song—do something productive and distracting—when the phone rang. And his heart actually jumped.

"Loser," he said under his breath, rolling his eyes. Still, he dropped the guitar on his bed rather quickly and scooped the phone up off the floor.

"Yeah?" he said into the receiver, tucking his free hand under his arm.

"Hey, it's me."

"Oh . . . hey, Tee," Conner said, his hopes dropping.

"What a greeting!" she said sarcastically.

"What's up?" Conner asked.

"I just wanted to see if you wanted to hang out tonight," Tia said. "I don't know what we're doing yet, but I'm sure it's going to be way fun."

Conner scoffed and sat down on his bed, running his hand over his shaggy brown hair. "Tee, I think you've done enough baby-sitting lately."

"Oh, come on. If it were baby-sitting, I'd be getting paid!" she joked.

"Thanks, but I kind of want to be alone tonight," Conner said. "I'll probably just go somewhere and listen to music or something."

"'Kay," Tia said. "But if you change your mind, give me a call."

"Later," Conner said. He clicked off the phone and dropped it on the bed next to him. Before long, he found himself staring at it again. Maybe he should have left a message. . . .

"All right, that's it," he said. He got up, grabbed his jacket from the back of his chair, and fled the room before he could make another stupid move.

* * *

I can't believe he's still trying to call me, Alanna thought, glaring at her telephone as she pulled her long auburn curls up into a bun at the back of her head. She'd finally had to take the phone off the hook to keep herself from losing it. Every time the phone rang these days, her shoulders tensed up, and each ring seemed to fray her nerves a little bit more as she waited for the machine to kick in.

He hadn't left a message this last time, but she was sure it had been him. None of her other friends ever missed the opportunity to leave a long, rambling message.

"He just doesn't get it," Alanna said aloud, pulling her hair out and starting over. "How could he possibly think I'm ever going to talk to him again after what he did?"

Groaning, Alanna walked over to her bed and flopped on top of her twisted bedspread facedown. Immediately her mind flashed back to that moment. The moment when everything had changed between her and Conner.

She saw the expressions on her parents' faces. The righteous pity in Conner's eyes. How could he look at her like that? She hadn't needed to be saved. All she'd wanted was to get away. He, of all people, should have been able to understand that. But no. Instead he brought the very people she'd wanted to get away from right to her door.

I'm never going to forgive him, she told herself, playing with the black fringe that edged her leopard-print throw pillow. *Besides, it's so uncool how he keeps calling. I mean, how pathetic is he?*

Her heart twisted in her chest at this thought, but she pushed it aside. She wasn't going to let herself feel anything for Conner. There was no point. It was over.

There was a knock at her bedroom door, and Alanna sat up automatically, pulling the pillow into her lap and continuing to fiddle with the fringe.

"Come in!" she called.

"Hi, honey," her mother said brightly as she entered the room. "What are you up to?"

"Not . . . much," Alanna said slowly, her eyebrows knitting together. Her mother was acting a bit too chipper for her taste. Maybe she'd had too much sugar in her tea this morning. But whatever it was that was making her mom grin like that, it did nothing but make Alanna suspicious. "What's up?" she asked.

"Well, I was thinking we should spend the day together tomorrow," Mrs. Feldman said, walking into the room and perching on the edge of her bed. Her hair was pulled back in a perfect low ponytail, and she was wearing a skirt. A skirt. On Saturday. How could Alanna possibly be related to this person?

"Just the two of us?" she asked. It came out

sounding totally negative, but she couldn't help it. This was all she needed right now. A full day of one-on-one lectures.

"Don't sound so tense," her mother said with a small laugh. "I'm not planning anything scary. We'll do something relaxing and fun. No stressful talk allowed. I promise."

"If you say so," Alanna said, drawing up her legs and crossing them in front of her. She still couldn't shake the thought that her mother was up to something. As long as she'd lived, Alanna was sure her mother had never suggested a day of bonding before.

"Good. It's going to be fun," her mother said, her features softening.

She patted Alanna's knee, and Alanna felt herself crack a smile as her mom got up and left the room, closing the door quietly behind her. Okay, so the whole situation was suspicious, but she couldn't help but be a little bit touched. Maybe her mom really was making an effort. And as dorky as it was, it kind of made Alanna feel good.

Melissa Fox pulled her car to a stop in front of Aaron Dallas's sprawling stucco ranch house and flipped down the visor to check her makeup in the mirror.

"Eyes . . . good. Cheeks . . . good," she said, tilting

11

her head from side to side. She grabbed her lip gloss out of her bag and touched up her lips, then fluffed her long brown hair and smiled. "Let the games begin," she said.

She pulled her shoulder bag off the passenger seat and climbed out of the car, taking a moment to smooth down the front of her floral sundress. Sure, it might be a bit much for a tutoring session, but she only had so many afternoons to make Aaron fall in love with her. She had to use everything she could.

The moment she had this thought, Melissa's stomach took a dangerous turn. Did she really want to go through with this? Sure, both Will and Cherie deserved some retaliation for everything they'd done to her in the past couple of weeks, but did she really want to sink to their level? Making the guy Cherie wanted fall in love with Melissa instead might be a bit over the top.

Melissa took a deep breath and thought back to the dance and how Will had humiliated her in front of the entire school. She recalled how devastated she'd felt when Cherie and the rest of her friends had basically turned their backs on her for no good reason. And that was all she needed to make herself move away from her car.

"Just stay cool," Melissa told herself, rolling back her shoulders as she walked up the front path and rang the doorbell. Aaron answered seconds later, and a wide grin spread across Melissa's face. "Hi, Aaron," she said smoothly.

"Hi, Melissa," he returned, taking a step back so that she could move into the foyer. "Thanks again for doing this."

"Oh, it's no problem," Melissa said, swinging her hair behind her shoulder. She looked Aaron up and down and realized it wasn't going to be at all hard to flirt with him. She'd always thought Aaron Dallas was good-looking, but today he looked particularly hot in a white T-shirt that showed off his surfer's tan and a pair of broken-in SVH soccer shorts. As always, his long blond bangs were hanging over his forehead and into his eyes in a seriously cute way.

"I figured we could work in the kitchen," Aaron said, tossing an apple from hand to hand as he led her through his spacious house. "It's not that comfortable, but I figure the less comfortable, the easier to concentrate on the evil Shakespeare."

"Kitchen's fine with me," Melissa said. Her heart was actually pounding as she settled into a chair across the table from Aaron. There were a lot of possible pitfalls to her plan. Not the least of which was the fact that Aaron was friends with Will. If the guy had any honor whatsoever, he might rebuff her advances before she even got started. But then again, teenage guys weren't particularly obsessed with honor. They were a bit more obsessed with girls.

"Before we start, I just wanted to tell you . . . I thought you were awesome in the game last night," Melissa said, blushing slightly. She glanced up at him through her lashes as if she was shy about complimenting him.

Aaron blushed himself, and his blue eyes brightened a bit. "Thanks," he said. "I guess I had a good night."

"Definitely," Melissa said. "You came *that* close to breaking the one-game scoring record."

"Well, maybe next time," Aaron said with a laugh. He shrugged as if it was all no big deal and took a huge bite out of his apple, but Melissa could tell he was really flattered she'd brought it up.

"This is going to sound stupid, but you did a great job last night too," he said as he chewed, leaning forward in his chair.

Melissa laughed and tucked her hair behind her ear. "Please. What, did you notice my basket toss or something?"

Aaron's blush deepened, and he shrugged again. "I don't know—you can just tell who knows what they're doing out there and who doesn't. And you're definitely one of the best on the squad."

"Thanks," Melissa said with a genuine smile.

Aaron crunched into his apple and gave her a quick wink before opening his textbook. "No problem," he said, tossing his head back quickly to get his hair out of his eyes.

As Melissa pulled her book out of her bag and started to dig for a pen, she had to struggle to keep herself from smiling triumphantly. Aaron was obviously up for flirting. And he was definitely easy to be with. This whole thing was going to be a lot simpler than she thought.

Cherie Reese

I know it sounds ridiculous, but I really think I'm in love with Aaron Dallas. I know, I know, I've never even kissed him, but this can't just be a crush. I've had a million crushes before, and none of them has ever felt like this. I want to know what the guy cares about, what he likes to eat for breakfast, what he thinks about before he goes to bed at night.

Okay, I'm not a stalker. I'm just in love.

And I'm so glad that Melissa's helping me. It was so cool of her to offer to spend time with him and find out more about him for me. What other friend would waste a few perfectly good afternoons studying just to help a girl out? Melissa Fox is the only one I can think of.

A lot of people think Melissa is only out for herself, but i've known her for a long time, and i know that there's no friend more loyal. She's a good person to have around . . . as long as she's on your side.

CHAPTER

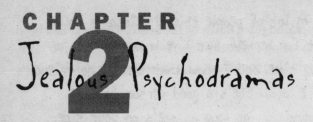

Jealous 2 Psychodramas

"This is not good. This is really, really, *really* not good," Jeremy Aames moaned to himself as he curled up in a fetal position on his bed on Saturday afternoon.

He'd never been so uncomfortable in his life. But uncomfortable was better than the total pain he'd been in a few hours before. And being able to lie still in his bed was a definite improvement on the constant bathroom runs he'd been taking in the wee hours of the morning. Jeremy had slept for about two hours, between 12 A.M. and 2 A.M., when he'd woken up in a cold sweat, his stomach trying to claw its way out of his body.

"I am never eating fish again," Jeremy told himself, squeezing his brown eyes shut and pulling his dark blue comforter up under his chin. "For as long as I live, I am done with seafood."

The night before, he and Jessica had decided to be adventurous and try a new all-you-can-eat seafood place down by the beach. The food had been amazing . . . at the time. But now he was pretty certain that something he'd eaten had given him a massive case of food poisoning.

Maybe I should call Jessica now, Jeremy thought, looking over at the bedside table, where the phone was sitting. He'd thought about calling her all morning to see if she was okay but had never thought he'd be able to stay on the phone long enough to get out the question.

Feeling beyond weak, Jeremy reached out one clammy hand and shakily picked up the cordless. He hit the speed-dial button for Jessica's number and lay back down on his side, resting the phone on his cheek. It rang four times before someone picked up, fumbled, and dropped the phone, then finally managed to speak.

"Hello?" Jessica croaked, her voice a harsh whisper. She sounded awful. She sounded even worse than he felt. Jeremy's heart squeezed. He'd really been hoping Jessica had escaped somehow.

"You too, huh?" Jeremy said.

"Jeremy, what did we do to ourselves?" she half moaned.

"I don't know," Jeremy said, trying to breathe evenly. "But mine's starting to get better. Is yours?"

"A little," Jessica said, managing a small laugh. "My insides are all on the outside now."

"I know the feeling," Jeremy said as his stomach gave an unsettling lurch. "Listen, feel better, okay? I'll try to call you again later."

"Okay. You too," Jessica said.

Jeremy clicked off the phone and turned onto his back, hoping the shift in position would help alleviate the pressure a bit. It didn't, but it did make it easier to breathe. There was a soft knock on the door, and Jeremy got an instant, comforting mental image of his mother, then felt like a total loser. He was eighteen years old. He didn't need his mother to look after him when he was sick. But still, it would have been nice if his whole family wasn't living miles away in Arizona. Jeremy would have felt much better if he was in his own bedroom instead of his friend Trent's older brother's room, with no one but Trent to take care of him.

Especially considering he and Trent Maynor weren't exactly friends at the moment.

"Come in," Jeremy said, his voice coming out all gravelly.

"Hey, man," Trent said, sticking his head into the room. "You all right?"

"Not exactly," Jeremy said, his jaw clenching. Every time he saw Trent, he got angry instantly. He still hadn't gotten over the fact that Trent had made a play for Jessica. If there was one thing Jeremy

20

couldn't tolerate, it was disloyalty. And from the tentative expression on Trent's face and the fact that he was still hovering over by the door, it was clear that Trent knew just how upset Jeremy still was.

"Anything I can do?" Trent asked, raising his eyebrows.

"No, man," Jeremy said. "I just want to be left alone."

Trent's whole face fell, and Jeremy's stomach responded with a little flop. Some added movement that his digestive system definitely didn't need right now. But it was hard not to react when Trent was upset. He looked like a little kid who'd just been told he couldn't go outside to play. Still, it wasn't Jeremy's problem. He wasn't the one who'd backstabbed his best friend.

"All right, well, just call me if you need anything," Trent said, his hand on the doorknob. "I'll be here."

Jeremy knew he should say thanks, but he didn't have it in him. Instead he just rolled over onto his side again, putting his back to the door, and closed his eyes. Maybe if he got some sleep, he'd feel better when he woke up.

Physically anyway.

Elizabeth stood against the wall underneath the deejay booth at the Riot on Saturday night, feeling

21

completely conspicuous. She seemed to be the only person in the packed club who was there alone. Jeff had asked her to come and hear him spin and hang out during his breaks, which had seemed like a great idea . . . when Jessica and Jeremy had agreed to come along. But once it became clear that neither one of them was going to be in the condition to party, Elizabeth had realized she was going to be spending most of the night by herself. And for some reason, it felt like all the people on the dance floor were looking at her—wondering who the lone loser was.

Okay, maybe if I move around, I won't stick out like such a sore thumb, Elizabeth thought. She pushed herself away from the wall and waved up at Jeff, motioning that she was going to go get a drink. Jeff smiled back and gave her a quick nod as he held his earphones up to one ear. Taking a deep breath, Elizabeth dove into the gyrating crowd on the dance floor and made her way to the other side as quickly as possible, and with only minor bruising.

The moment she emerged near the bar, however, Elizabeth saw something that made her heart catch in her throat. She wasn't the only one who was here alone. Conner was sitting at the end of the bar, slouched on his stool, looking seriously depressed. And none of his friends were anywhere in sight.

For a moment Elizabeth considered going over

there and talking to him. He looked like he was in serious wallow mode. But then, she and Conner hadn't been friends in a very long time. She wasn't sure he would look at her, let alone talk to her. At this point she couldn't even remember what it *felt* like to talk to him.

Elizabeth was about to move away and head for the bathroom when the bartender handed Conner a drink. And it wasn't a soda. Elizabeth went rigid with fear. It couldn't be . . . could it? Before she could think it through, she was making a beeline for the bar. She knew he was going to hate her, but there was no way she was just going to stand there and watch him get drunk. By the time she got to his side, Elizabeth was shaking with nerves, and he was lifting the glass to his lips.

"Do you really want to do that?" she asked, her pulse pounding.

Conner slowly looked over at her, and the moment he saw who was talking to him, his eyes hardened. "I'm thirsty," he said flatly. Then he downed half the contents of the glass.

Elizabeth's mouth dropped open, and she laid her hand on the bar for support. She couldn't believe this was happening. After everything he'd been through . . . after everything *they'd* been through . . . he was really just going to sit here and toss back alcohol like it was no big deal?

23

"Conner, what are you—"

"Seltzer?" Conner asked, tipping the glass in her direction.

Elizabeth's heart hit the floor along with all of the blood in her face. For a moment she actually felt like she was going to die of embarrassment. *Goody-goody Liz does it again.*

"Thanks for your concern," Conner said with a hard smirk. He gulped down the rest of his drink and slapped the empty glass on the bar. "Glad you have so much faith in me."

Elizabeth stood there a moment as it slowly sank in just how big of a fool she'd made of herself. She opened her mouth to apologize, but her voice nearly choked her. Still, she managed to get a few words through.

"I'm sorry, Conner . . . really. I—" She paused and swallowed, her throat completely dry. "I'm such an idiot. I just . . . I know this sounds stupid, but I just don't want anything to happen to you. I just . . . I don't know." She brought her hand to her forehead, wishing she could verbalize what she was feeling, but it was pointless because she had no idea what it was she was feeling.

"I'm sorry," she said again, looking directly into his steady green gaze. He didn't blink, didn't move, didn't say a word. So instead of torturing herself further, Elizabeth turned to go.

*　　　*　　　*

"All right, so are we seeing *Deep Space* or *For the Love of You*?" Will Simmons asked Melissa as they stood in an impossibly long line outside the movie theater on Saturday night.

"What do you think?" Melissa shot back, looking up at him with serious sarcasm in her ice blue eyes.

"Right. *For the Love of You* it is," Will said with a chuckle, rubbing his hands together. He didn't really care what they saw as long as he got his large popcorn and peanut M&Ms. He could sit through pretty much anything if he had his junk food. Of course, the night would be perfect if the sappy love story Melissa wanted to see just happened to be sold out by the time they got to the ticket window. Will studied the line in front of them, trying to count how many people he thought might go in for a mushy movie.

"So, I had my first tutoring session with Aaron today," Melissa said, looping her arm around his as they inched forward.

"Oh, yeah?" Will said. He'd thought he'd heard someone up ahead say something was sold out, and he was trying to hear what it was.

"Yeah. And I think it went really well. Thanks for asking," Melissa said, nudging him with her elbow.

Will blinked and looked down at her, realizing from her tone that she was irritated. Better pay

25

attention. "That's great. Aaron's a great guy."

"He is. It's just . . . " Melissa bit her lip, and her face scrunched up hesitantly. "When I brought up Cherie's name, he seemed totally uninterested. Do you think you could tell me a little bit more about him? I want to give Cherie something to work with here, and Aaron was not helpful."

Will ran his hand through his blond hair and blew out a sigh. He'd actually forgotten that this whole tutoring thing was just a cover so that Melissa could help Cherie snag Aaron. It all seemed a little bit juvenile and circumspect to him. If Cherie liked Aaron, why didn't she just ask him out? Why did Will always have to get sucked into everything?

"I don't know, Liss," Will said. "He's a guy. He likes sports. He likes to win. What else can I tell you?"

Melissa rolled her eyes in exasperation. "Um . . . *anything?*" she prodded. "I mean, the guy is your *friend.* Don't you know anything about him?"

"Well, it's not like we sit around in the locker room discussing our deepest feelings," Will said with a shrug as the line inched along. "I gotta be honest, Liss, I don't really understand why you're doing this. They're either attracted to each other or not. How is your tutoring him going to change that?"

Melissa's cheeks turned crimson. She glanced away, and Will knew he was walking on thin ice. She was starting to get seriously annoyed. And if she was seriously annoyed, he could kiss away any chance at a pleasant evening.

"What about music?" Melissa said, throwing one hand up. "Do you know what kind of music he likes?"

Will grinned, a little thread of relief running through his veins. "That I know. He's a rap fiend," he said with a laugh. "All the SVH guys are always on his case because he used to be all about country-western and now it's like he'll only buy CDs that have parental advisories on them."

"Rap, okay," Melissa said with a thoughtful nod, staring at some point over his shoulder. "That's a start."

Just before they got to the ticket booth, Melissa touched his arm, stopping him, and looked him in the eye. "I want you to find out everything you can about Aaron over the next couple of days, okay?" she asked.

"Sure," Will said, pulling his wallet out of the back pocket of his jeans. But inside he felt a little pang of irritation. It was nice that Melissa wanted to help Cherie, but he'd rather just be left out of his girlfriend's little schemes. Nine times out of ten, they did not end well.

"Two for *For the Love of You*," Melissa told the girl behind the glass.

"Sold out," the girl answered in a bored voice.

Yes! Will thought, trying not to smile. This night was looking up.

Conner sat there for a split second, jaw clenched, hand wrapped tightly around his empty glass, guilt seeming to seep into his body through every last pore. Elizabeth was barely three steps away when he decided he couldn't take it anymore.

"Liz," he said quietly. Maybe she wouldn't hear him over the music and she'd keep walking. That way he'd know he tried, but he wouldn't have to deal with talking to her.

But of course, she turned around the moment he said her name, her blue-green eyes filled with hope.

"Sorry," he said. "Long day."

"It's all right," Elizabeth said, pulling on the hem of her frilly, almost low cut red blouse. She took a tentative step toward him. "I really didn't mean anything."

"I know," Conner said. He saw her eyeing the stool next to him and decided it would be easier to let her stay than try to tell her to go away without offending her all over again. "You can sit," he said.

"Thanks," Elizabeth said with a smile.

She slid onto the stool and crossed her legs, her skirt riding up to expose a couple of extra inches of her tanned leg. Conner smiled too. He could remember a time when just that simple movement would have made him sick with desire for her, but all he felt now was a slight twinge of interest, like he would with any half-dressed, beautiful girl that walked into the room. It really was amazing how attraction came and went.

"So . . . I might as well tell you . . . I heard about you and Alanna," Elizabeth said.

Conner's heart responded with a painful thump. What he wouldn't give to have Alanna sitting here right now. Maybe even wearing the same outfit. She would look damn hot in that blouse. . . .

"I'm really sorry," Elizabeth said sincerely.

Conner shrugged and tipped the glass to his lips again, getting the last couple of drops. "It's okay," he said. *Let's just talk about something else,* he suggested mentally.

"So, did you write your piece for creative writing yet?" Elizabeth asked, as if she was reading his mind. Then again, he knew she could read him pretty well. It was one thing that had always both annoyed and intrigued him about her.

"I'm working on it," he said. "You?"

"I've got a first draft," Elizabeth said, pushing a lock of blond hair behind her ear. "It basically sucks."

"I doubt that," Conner said with a smirk.

Elizabeth grinned and looked at him out of the corner of her eye. "Did you just compliment me?" she asked slyly.

"Don't press it," Conner said, chuckling.

He raised a hand at the bartender as Elizabeth started to explain the concept of her short story. As his glass was refilled, Conner realized that he was really listening to Elizabeth. That he was actually interested in what she had to say. His mind wasn't constantly wandering off to her lips, her eyes, her skin. It was amazing how much easier it was to talk to her when he wasn't salivating over her the whole time.

She was still one of the hottest girls he'd ever known, but his heart and everything else were focused elsewhere.

Then, out of nowhere, Elizabeth started to stammer, and she kept looking over Conner's shoulder. He finally turned to see what was bothering her and saw her boyfriend weaving his way across the dance floor toward them. Jeff something or other. At least, Conner thought he was Elizabeth's boyfriend. He'd seen her in the hall with him a couple of times, but that was basically all he knew. That, and the fact that the guy looked like a total tool.

Conner had started to turn his attention back to Elizabeth when he noticed Jeff notice him, and the smile fell right off Jeff's face. Every muscle in Conner's body tensed as he wondered if this guy was going to make a scene. Most boyfriends seemed to have a problem with Conner talking to their women, and Conner had been in a lot of altercations because of it. He had no idea why the guys started with him, of course. It wasn't like it was his fault if their girlfriends were attracted to him.

"Hey!" Elizabeth said a bit too brightly when Jeff finally reached her side. She was blushing like mad, and she definitely looked guilty. Conner's back went rigid. If Elizabeth was going to *act* like there was something going on, he should definitely be ready to defend himself.

"Hey, yourself," Jeff said, sliding his arm around Elizabeth's shoulders.

"Jeff, this is Conner. Conner, Jeff," Elizabeth said quickly.

"Nice to meet you," Jeff said with a nod.

"Yeah, you too," Conner answered, glancing quickly at Jeff over his shoulder. The guy was acting friendly enough, but it was clear from the hard look in his eyes and the possessive grip he had on Elizabeth that he wasn't happy with the situation.

Conner pushed himself away from the bar and tossed down a couple of dollars. "I'll see ya," he said to Elizabeth as he moved away. He didn't feel like getting involved in any jealous psychodramas right now. Especially when he wasn't interested in the girl in question.

As he made his way to the door, Conner felt the ire start to build up in his veins. He was just *talking* to the girl. Did that really have to be so complex? But of course it did. She was an ex. So of course things weren't going to be cut-and-dried. He should never even bother trying to be friends with someone he once dated. He had enough to worry about.

Of course, that would mean you'll never be friends with Alanna, a little voice in his head reminded him as he shoved his way into the cool night air. Conner paused and took a deep breath. That was something he just could not accept.

Elizabeth Wakefield

What a night. Seriously. It's so bizarre how you can leave your house thinking that you know exactly what to expect out of an evening, and then something totally random happens. This morning if you had told me I'd be sitting at a bar, chatting with Conner, I would have told you to go get a CAT scan.

And what was even more surprising was how comfortable it was. After the initial mortification, of course. Once we got to talking, it was great. It was so normal. I don't think I've ever felt so comfortable talking to him before in my life. I can't stop thinking about it. It was just so . . . I don't know . . . perfect.

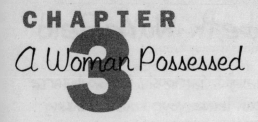

CHAPTER 3

A Woman Possessed

When Jeremy woke up on Sunday morning, he couldn't move. He was so exhausted from all the trauma his body had been through the day before, he could barely lift his head from the pillow to check the time. All he'd consumed in the last twenty-four hours was water and one cracker. There was no way he was going to have the energy to get out of bed.

Summoning up a bit of strength, Jeremy lifted his hand and pushed the bottle of Pepto-Bismol, the water glass, and the crumpled bag of crackers out of the way so that he could see his clock.

"Nine-thirty?" Jeremy groaned aloud, squinting at the big, blurry digital numbers. He dropped his head back onto the pillow. He was supposed to be at work at House of Java in an hour. Like that was ever going to happen. Just the thought of smelling coffee made his stomach turn. And in his condition, there was no way he could work a slow night shift at the coffee bar, let alone deal with the insane crush Sunday mornings usually brought.

Taking a deep breath, Jeremy reached for the phone and shakily dialed the number for the coffee shop. He closed his eyes as it rang and almost passed out again before someone picked up on the sixth or seventh ring.

"House of Java!"

It was his manager, Ally Scott. And she already sounded annoyed. Her voice got all nasal and pinched whenever something was wrong.

"Ally? It's Jeremy," he said. His voice came out like a croak.

"Oh, don't even tell me," she said, her words laced with anger.

Jeremy's forehead creased with confusion. What was going on? "Listen, I just called to tell you I can't make it in today. I'm really sick, and I—"

"That is just *so* convenient!" Ally said with a sarcastic snort. Jeremy could hear the dinging of the cash register and the slushing of the cappuccino machine in the background. Ally was obviously working the counter when she should have been back in the office. "Guess who else just called in sick, Jeremy?"

Then it hit him. "Jessica!" he said, bringing his hand to his head. He'd completely forgotten they were both supposed to work that morning. Ally was probably freaking with two people bailing on the busiest day of the week.

"Bingo!" Ally said. The cash-register drawer slammed. "So, what are you guys doing today? Hitting the beach? It's a beautiful day for it."

"Ally, you don't understand," Jeremy said. Something moved, and he looked up to find Trent leaning in the doorway of his room. Jeremy looked away and kept talking, wishing Trent would just leave. This really wasn't any of his business. "Jessica and I—"

"No, Jeremy, *you* don't understand," Ally said. "Even after two years of working here, you obviously don't get that I need you on Sunday. I need as many people as I can get on Sunday. But because two of my best workers also happen to be lovebirds, I get screwed."

"I'm sorry," Jeremy said patiently, even though the guilt was starting to weigh on him already. "We really are sick."

"Fine. If that's the story you want to stick with, there's nothing I can say about it." With that, she slammed down the phone so hard, it hurt Jeremy's eardrum.

Heaving a sigh, Jeremy hung up the phone and placed it back on his bedside table. His hand was shaking from lack of food. He tucked it under the covers and fell back into his pillows, feeling exhausted all over again.

"Was that Ally?" Trent asked.

Jeremy stared at the ceiling. He did not want to have this conversation with Trent right now, but explaining felt easier than shutting him out and possibly arguing.

"Yeah. Jessica and I both called in sick, and she doesn't believe us," he said. There. End of story. Trent could go away now.

"Can't she call in someone else to cover?" Trent asked, crossing his arms over the front of his Big Mesa sweatshirt.

"Apparently not," Jeremy said. It wasn't like there was anything Trent could do about it, so why did he want all the gory details? "People don't like to work Sundays unless they absolutely have to."

"I get it," Trent said. "Well, is there anything I can do?"

Yeah. Go away, Jeremy thought. But he didn't say it. He probably couldn't have if he'd wanted to. It would have made him feel guilty, and he'd already had enough of that particular emotion for one morning.

"No, thanks," he said. "I think I'm going to go back to sleep."

Trent stood there for a moment, then seemed to realize that Jeremy wasn't going to say anything more. "Okay," he said. "Feel better." Then he pulled the door closed and walked away.

Jeremy just lay there, thinking over the conversation with Ally and the tension between him and Trent. Considering he'd only been awake for about five minutes, he was pretty sure this day couldn't get much worse.

Alanna stared down at the clear glass plate in front of her and moved a piece of lettuce from one side of it to the other. Then she moved it back. This poor piece of lettuce had already been displaced a countless number of times, but Alanna couldn't help it. She didn't want to *eat* her salad, but she had to make it look like she was doing *something*.

"Are you okay, Alanna?" her mother asked, the perfectly plucked and filled-in eyebrows coming together over her nose. "You've barely eaten a bite of your salad."

Probably because I hate vegetables, Alanna thought with a sigh. She should have gotten the burger. She knew she should have. But she didn't want to cause waves with her mother. Not on their bonding day. So she'd opted for starvation instead. Brilliant.

"I'm not really hungry, I guess," Alanna said, forcing a small smile as her stomach let out an audible growl.

Alanna looked around the café—one of her mom's favorites—at the other diners. The place was bright, cheerful, and pristine, with white tablecloths and fresh flowers on the tables. It was filled almost entirely with women, all of whom were surrounded by shopping bags. All except Alanna and her mother, but only because they'd left their mountains of purchases in the car. Alanna almost winced when she thought of all the clothing she'd just allowed her mother to buy for her—none of which she could ever imagine herself wearing.

Once Alanna had figured out that her mother's idea of bonding involved dragging her to all Mrs. Feldman's favorite shops and now her favorite restaurant, Alanna had decided it would be easier to just cave in and go with the flow. She didn't have enough energy to spend a whole day fighting. So now she was the proud owner of a new pastel wardrobe.

"I'm so glad you decided to get that pink sweater," her mother said with a grin, as if she were reading Alanna's mind. "It really is your color."

Yeah, right, Alanna thought. She'd wear the pink cashmere cardigan the day her mother went out to a charity event in fishnet stockings.

"So, did anything interesting happen in school this week?" Alanna's mother asked as she touched her napkin to the corners of her mouth.

Alanna smiled. A lot interesting had happened, actually. Two guys from the basketball team had been caught with pot in the bathroom, and one of the girls from Alanna's art class had had a little breakdown in the middle of a pottery lesson and smashed her work against the wall, but Alanna knew her mother didn't actually want to hear anything *interesting*. She wanted to hear about Alanna's grades. If there were any tests. And if Alanna had passed those tests.

"Not really," Alanna said with a shrug. She *had* had two big tests this past week, but she didn't have the grades back yet, and she wasn't that confident about them.

"Report cards should be coming out soon, right?" her mother asked, trying to sound totally nonchalant.

"Probably," Alanna said, knowing full well that the marking period ended in a couple of weeks.

Her mother paused and rested her forearms on the edge of the table, just above the elbow. Actually putting her elbows on the table would have been a sacrilege. She scrunched up her face in a poor imitation of concentration. "Now, remind me, do they send those home with the students, or do they get mailed?"

Alanna felt her cheeks heat up, and she slouched down a bit in her chair. "Don't worry, Mom. I'll bring my report card home."

"Alanna, I wasn't implying that—"

"Yes, you were," Alanna said firmly, feeling humiliated and angry at the same time. "Just forget it." She forced herself to sit up straight again and took a bite of her food. "What are we doing next?" she asked, hoping against hope that her mom would say they were headed home. At this point Alanna would give just about anything to be anywhere but here.

Her mother rolled back her shoulders and looked down at her food for a moment, regaining her composure after the near argument. "We're going to the Day Spa!" she said brightly. "I booked two full treatments—mud baths, facials, massages. It's going to be great."

"Yeah . . . great," Alanna said. She could just imagine what she was in for—some snooty women touching her all over the place, resenting her the entire time for having so much money—and the gall to waste it on such frivolous crap. Alanna wouldn't blame them for hating her either. Just the thought made her skin crawl.

Conner would laugh so hard if he heard this, she thought suddenly. She found herself conjuring up an image of Conner's face with his telltale smirk. Then her heart sank, and as quickly as the image appeared, she brushed it away.

Mother-daughter bonding, she told herself. *Focus here. Maybe this is exactly what you need. Maybe all this superficial stuff will take your mind off Conner.*

Unfortunately, she had the feeling that all it was going to do was make her long for him more.

*   *   *

41

Melissa walked into the bright, neon-lit MusicWorld store in the Valley Mall and automatically headed to the left side of the store, where they kept the pop and dance albums. As soon as she realized what she was doing, she laughed at herself. It was total force of habit. Melissa had been coming to this store her entire life, and she was pretty sure she'd never ventured *out* of the pop and dance sections.

But she was here on a mission. And that mission was to find out everything she could about rap—and considering she knew less than nothing and wanted to be able to talk about it with someone who was a rap fiend, she could be here for a while.

Glancing around the store, Melissa's eyes fell on the bright red sign that indicated the rap section. She wandered over to the middle aisle and tried to look like she knew what she was doing as she flipped through a few CDs. A couple of guys dressed in head-to-toe black who were toting about five CDs each looked her up and down and laughed as they walked by. Melissa looked over her capri pants and pink T-shirt and realized that she might have been better off dressing a little less like a cheerleader. As it was, she was completely conspicuous.

She glanced around and caught a glimpse of another girl, who was listening to a pair of headphones at the rap listening booth. Her back was to Melissa, but she had on a baseball cap, a pair of jeans, and a white T-shirt. Not *so* different from Melissa. She lifted her chin and stared down the cacklers, who were still giggling at the end of the aisle. For all they knew, she could be the biggest rap fan ever. They could just kiss her—

"Melissa!"

She jumped at the sound of her name and looked back at the baseball-cap girl. It was Cherie. No wonder Melissa had thought she looked like someone she could be friends with.

"Hey!" Melissa said, slightly baffled. "What are you doing here?"

Cherie blushed as she walked over to Melissa. She was carrying a couple of rap CDs, and she held them up for Melissa to see.

"I'm actually shopping for Aaron," she said with an uncertain smile. "His birthday is this Wednesday, and I wanted to get him something." She shrugged one shoulder and turned the CDs over to read the song lists.

"Oh, really?" Melissa asked. She was a bit taken off guard. Why hadn't *she* known that Aaron's birthday was this week? She obviously had to brush up on her fact-finding skills.

"Yeah. We're going to go out to celebrate on Tuesday since he's going out with his family on Wednesday," Cherie said, biting her lip.

Melissa felt the color rise up in her cheeks. Cherie was going out on a date with Aaron? For his birthday? Why the heck had the girl wanted her help? She seemed to be doing more than fine on her own.

"Wow, Cherie. I guess you don't need me anymore," Melissa said, crossing her arms over her waist.

"I don't know," Cherie said with a shrug. She looked down at her feet, and Melissa realized she'd never seen the normally confident Cherie look so vulnerable. "I mean, *I* asked *him* out. And I kind of got the feeling he was only saying yes to be polite, you know?" When she looked up again, her green eyes were begging for Melissa to say something reassuring. It was all Melissa could do to keep from laughing. So Cherie didn't quite have Aaron wrapped around her finger . . . yet. There was still a chance.

"I'm sure that's not true," Melissa said, touching Cherie's arm. Then she looked down at the CDs Cherie was holding and winced. "Are you sure you want to get him those, though?"

"Why? Are they no good?" Cherie asked. "The guy behind the counter said they were brand-new and were getting really good reviews."

"Maybe, but do you really want to get him rap?" Melissa asked, tilting her head. "That's kind of risky. I'd go with classic-rock CDs. All guys like classic rock."

She walked over to the end of the aisle where they displayed the classic-rock selections and picked up *The Best of The Who*. "Get him this," Melissa said. "It's a no-brainer."

Cherie adjusted the strap of her bag on her shoulder and eyed Melissa, confused. "I don't know. I'm pretty sure Aaron likes rap."

"Pretty sure?" Melissa asked, leveling Cherie with her best challenging stare. *Do you really want to take the chance?* her eyes asked. *This is the first present you'll ever get the guy. It means everything.*

She could practically see Cherie waffling before her eyes. She shifted from foot to foot, deliberated, and finally put the rap CDs back on the shelf.

"Maybe you're right," Cherie said, stepping up next to Melissa and taking the Who CD from her. Her expression was the picture of uncertainty as she looked it over, but she started to walk up toward the register.

"I am," Melissa said with a smile, putting her hand on Cherie's back. "Trust me."

I can't believe this is happening to me. I can't believe this is happening to me. Why? Why? Why? Why? Why?

Tears of pain streaked down Alanna's cheeks as she inched her way across the sidewalk toward her mother's waiting car. One of the workers from the Day Spa hovered over her, asking her if there was anything she could do, but Alanna just wanted her to go away so she could suffer in peace. Her whole body was covered with angry hives—a reaction to the full-body mask she'd been immersed in for fifteen minutes.

"I'm so sorry," the girl, who was about Alanna's size but a few years older, said for the hundredth time. "We use avocado in all our mud treatments. If only we'd known you were allergic—"

"Oh, you're blaming *us* now? That's just fine!" Alanna's mother said sarcastically as she got out of the car, letting it idle. She came around the front and opened the passenger door for Alanna. "You people should provide your clients with ingredient lists. I'm appalled that this happened."

The girl cowered in the face of Mrs. Feldman's rage. Alanna's mom was petite and normally refined, but when she got angry, no one wanted to be in her way.

"I didn't mean that," the girl said. "I'm sorry if I—"

"You'll be hearing from my lawyer," Alanna's mother spat, putting her hand on Alanna's back.

"Ow! Mom!" Alanna shouted, wincing from the pain. Even through the thick white robe she was wearing, the pressure from her mother's hand sent her reeling.

"Sorry, sweetie," her mother said.

Alanna climbed into the car and sat down gingerly, her hives painfully swollen. Her mother took a few more minutes to lace into the poor, innocent spa worker, and Alanna sat there, seething. Here she was, in desperate need of a hospital, and her mother was taking time out to throw her weight around. Typical.

Finally her mother got in behind the wheel and slammed the door. Then she gunned the engine and took off, speeding down the street like a woman possessed. Alanna tried to sit as perfectly still as possible even as the car lurched and wove its way through traffic. Every time she rubbed up against anything—the seat, the stick shift, the door—she wanted to scream from the pain.

"Honey, I am so sorry," her mother said, now near tears herself as she rushed Alanna to the hospital. "I had no idea. Who puts avocado in *mud?*"

"It's okay," Alanna said, sniffling. She couldn't even use a tissue because she couldn't move her arms. "You didn't know."

She stared out the window, trying to concentrate on the scenery flying by instead of on the pain. Back when she was three years old, Alanna and her parents had discovered the hard way that Alanna had a violent allergy to avocado when she'd broken out in hives after eating a salad on a trip to wine country. Since then she hadn't had one outbreak. She was always careful to make sure everything she ordered hadn't even *touched* an avocado—even this morning when she'd ordered her salad. How could this have happened?

"I'm so sorry," her mother kept saying, her eyes glued to the road. "All I wanted was for you and me to spend some quality time together. I promise you, Alanna, I did not take you out today with the intent of torturing you."

"I know, Mom," Alanna said through her tears. She did believe her mother, but she wished the woman would stop talking. Having to answer her just made the whole situation even more uncomfortable.

I wish Conner were here, she thought, a new wave of self-pitying tears brimming over. She knew she would feel so much better if he were at the hospital to hold her hand. If she could just look at him, she knew she'd feel like everything was going to be all right. He'd always had that effect on her.

But it wasn't going to happen. She was never going to feel that comfort again. And it was all Conner's fault.

Why did he have to go and mess everything up?

Will Simmons

The thing about Melissa is that even though in most ways she's more predictable than anyone I've ever known—sometimes it's scary how well I know her—she still manages to surprise me sometimes.

Ever since we got back together after the whole Erika Brooks thing, I've been waiting for the guilt trips to start. But they haven't. She's really let it go, something I didn't think was humanly possible for Melissa.

So maybe this time we actually have a chance to get it right.

melissa fox

I think I was meant to get revenge on Will and Cherie. I mean, it's all working out so perfectly, it's like fate is helping me out here. I'm going to make them pay, and I'm going to do it right.

Trent Maynor

Ten (Dumb) Ways to Get Jeremy to Talk to Me Again

10. Get us paired up for the next science project
9. Bring him to Mexico so he'd have to use me as a translator (his Spanish stinks)
8. Sit on the end of his bed and stare at him until he caves
7. Find that piece of paper we signed when we were five swearing we'd never get mad at each other no matter what
6. Get him so sick that he needs to rely on me for survival—oh, wait, that didn't work
5. Get Jessica to agree not to talk to him until he talks to me
4. Get Jessica to agree not to kiss him until he talks to me
3. Have his little sisters call him and

ask him to talk to me—he can't
resist them
2. Start systematically stealing his
stuff and don't give it back until he
forgives me
1. Turn back time and not come on
to Jessica

The moment Trent walked into House of Java on Sunday morning, he knew he'd made the right decision. The place was the picture of chaos. Ally Scott and her sister, Corey, were behind the counter, tripping over each other as they dealt with a long line of caffeine-deprived customers. Meanwhile the big blond guy . . . Danny was his name, as Trent recalled . . . was engaged in a losing battle with an obviously malfunctioning cappuccino machine. Trent made his way over to the end of the counter and waited for somebody to notice him.

No one did. They were too busy trying to hold the place together.

"Ally!" Trent said when she turned away from the register for a split second.

"Jeremy's not here," she said, glancing at him reproachfully as if he was the one who'd left her short-handed. Then she ducked under the counter to get something out of one of the cabinets. "You have to wait in line like everybody else," she said, her voice muffled since her head was buried.

"I don't want coffee," Trent said when she stood up again. "I'm here to help. I came in Jeremy's place." Ally let out a noise that sounded somewhat like a strangled laugh. "Right," she said. "Like what I really need right now is a totally inexperienced worker behind this counter. Tell Jeremy I said nice try."

"You clearly need *someone*," Trent said, raising his eyebrows as a crowd of well-dressed ladies walked through the door and joined the already noisy crowd. He could tell some of the people waiting were starting to get annoyed. They were shifting from foot to foot, sighing, standing on their tiptoes to see what was going on. Any second, Ally was going to have a riot on her hands.

"Thanks anyway," Ally said. She grabbed a cup and stuck it under the nozzle of one of the coffee machines. Then a surfer over by the sugar-and-milk station yelled out that there was no Equal left, and she turned quickly, moving her hand under the hot stream of coffee.

"Ow!" she shouted. The cup dropped to the floor, splattering coffee everywhere as she clung to her burned hand. Luckily the cup was paper, so there was no shattering involved. Ally kicked the cup in frustration and shoved her hand into the sink, turning on the cold-water faucet. Then she looked up at Trent through watery eyes. "Do you even know how to make a latte?" she asked.

"Uh . . . no. But I can clean up," Trent said, looking around at the tables. Most of them were littered with crumpled napkins, crumbs, and spills. The place was trashed. "I'll take out the garbage, fill up the sugar dispensers . . . whatever."

Ally looked around at the mob of customers waiting to be served and groaned. "Okay, fine," she said. She wiped off her hands and started filling a new coffee cup. "All the supplies are in the back. Let me know if there's anything you can't find."

"Cool," Trent said, coming around the counter.

"Hey. What's your name again?" Ally asked, stopping Trent as he pushed his way through the swinging doors into the back room.

"Trent Maynor," he said with a laugh. "Jeremy's my . . . he's my best friend." *Or was,* he added silently.

"So, Trent, what'd he do, bribe you?" Ally asked, handing the coffee to an older gentleman and pushing a few buttons on the cash register.

"Actually, I owe him one," Trent said, half smiling at the total understatement. "And he said you really needed someone, so . . ."

Ally cracked a grin and shook her head. "Well, thanks for coming," she said as she pushed a stray strand of straight brown hair back into her baseball cap. "I hope Jeremy appreciates what a good friend he has."

Trent's heart twisted in his chest, and he glanced down for a moment. "Yeah . . . we'll see," he said. Then he pushed through the doors and into the back room before Ally could ask him what he meant.

"Thank you, Ms. Rollins," Mr. Quigley said as Enid finished reading her short-short story on Monday afternoon. "That was very good work."

Enid ducked her head and sat down at her desk in the front row, looking relieved. Elizabeth smiled. She knew how that felt. Before class she'd been completely nervous about reading her assignment aloud, just as she always was, but ever since she'd finished, she'd been sitting in a state of stress-free euphoria. She loved that rush she always got after she finished doing something she'd been dreading.

"Let's see . . . who's the next victim?" the teacher said, mulling over the class list on the clipboard in front of him. "Mr. McDermott?" he said, looking up toward the back corner where Conner always sat. "Care to take a shot?"

Elizabeth sat straight up in her seat as Conner slowly lifted himself out of his chair and strolled to the front of the room. Her heart started to pound in her ears, and she rolled her eyes at herself. What was the big deal? It was just Conner. It wasn't like she was interested in him again or anything.

She took a deep breath and told herself to chill. So what if he looked amazing today? So what if she'd been thinking about him ever since the conversation they'd had on Saturday night? She couldn't help it. It had just been so . . . nice. And it wasn't as if she'd been *daydreaming* about him per se. She'd simply been wondering if he'd ever finished his piece for class. She was merely interested. On a friendly level.

"This is called 'The Lost Guitar,'" Conner said, leaning back casually against Quigley's desk. He glanced up at the classroom, and his eyes locked with Elizabeth's for a split second. She blushed immediately, and he looked down again and started to read.

What is wrong with me? Elizabeth thought, trying to focus on what Conner was reading instead of on her embarrassing blush. *His eyes just happened to fall on you, that's all,* she told herself.

". . . it was precious, beautiful, sonorous. The perfect instrument. In the wide world there was no match," Conner read, his eyes now glued to the page in front of him. "But as time wore on, the musician's eyes turned to other enticements. Electric models . . . bright colors . . . sleek shapes. The precious guitar lay forgotten, abandoned . . . alone."

Elizabeth sat, transfixed by the deep tones of Conner's voice. He was reading with so much feeling. Not that she was surprised. Conner's emotions pretty much only came out when he was reading or singing. But this particular story obviously meant a lot to him. She could tell by the way he was clutching the paper and by the fact that he refused to look up.

". . . when the musician was old, he remembered the precious guitar. He went to look for it, but to no avail. He ransacked his house, his studio, his yard and garage and car. And with each failed search his heart split open a bit wider. The guitar was gone. And it wasn't until he realized he would never be able to play it again. Never be able to strum its strings or touch its neck. It wasn't until he realized that it was gone forever that the musician knew how much he loved that guitar. And he sat alone in his studio and wept."

Conner glanced up when he finished reading. Everyone was totally silent.

"That's it," he said. Then he walked back to his desk and flopped down in his seat, scraping back the chair. The noise seemed to wake everyone up, and there was suddenly a lot of movement—people shifting in their seats, flipping papers, clearing their throats.

As Quigley called on the next student, Elizabeth couldn't move a muscle. Had she really heard what she thought she just heard? That story . . . it was a metaphor. She was sure of it. A musician who lost the one guitar he loved? Who tried out other fancy guitars but just wanted his first guitar back? Who finally went to find his first love but discovered it was gone forever?

Conner was the musician, and Elizabeth was the guitar! She had to be. Why else would he have looked at her that way before he started reading? He'd wanted her to realize that the piece was for her.

Before Elizabeth could even decide how she felt about all this, the bell rang and everyone jumped up from their desks. Elizabeth grabbed her stuff and walked to the front of the room to wait for Conner. She had no idea what she was going to say, but she had to say *something*. If she didn't, she was going to burst from curiosity.

Conner glanced up at her as he emerged from his row and clearly realized she was waiting for him. He stuck his free hand in the pocket of his jacket and walked over to her.

"Hey," he said, barely meeting her eyes.

"Hey," she answered with a smile. "I . . . I really liked your piece. It was . . ." *It was what? Interesting? Beautiful? Totally transparent?*

Elizabeth simply shrugged, at a complete loss. What was she supposed to do? Just tell him she knew what he was trying to say? Then he would ask her what she thought, and she had no idea what she thought. Maybe waiting for him hadn't been the best idea after all.

"Thanks," Conner said. Then he finally looked at her, his green eyes seeming to bore into hers. "I wasn't sure what you'd think."

Elizabeth blushed again, and her smile only widened. For Conner, those few words were enough to confirm her suspicions. He'd been thinking about her when he wrote the piece—wondering how she'd feel about it. And he'd never admit that to her unless he wanted her to know what she meant to him.

I don't believe it, she thought. *It really* is *about me.* Then, without another word, Conner slipped through the door and out into the hallway, leaving Elizabeth floating behind him.

This was unbelievable. After all this time was it really possible that Conner still wanted her? Considering the way their relationship ended, Elizabeth definitely wouldn't have minded Conner doing a little pining for her. It would be like evening the score.

But how do you *feel about* him? a little voice in her mind asked. Shaking her head, Elizabeth chose to ignore it. It didn't matter how she felt about Conner—all she knew was that she liked this excited little feeling in her stomach . . . and thinking about it too much would definitely make it go away.

She turned on her heel and took off for her locker, deciding instead to go over Conner's story again in her mind. *And he sat alone in his studio and wept* . . . Elizabeth almost laughed aloud. This was almost too good to be true.

As Will finished changing back into his clothes after gym class on Monday afternoon, he kept glancing over at Aaron Dallas, who was talking basketball with a couple of his teammates. Normally Will would be right there in the middle of the conversation, debating over potential district MVPs, but today he was too busy thinking. How was he supposed to get Aaron to tell him all the stuff Melissa and Cherie wanted to know about him without looking like an idiot?

"See ya later," Aaron said as Todd Wilkins grabbed his backpack and headed out of the locker room. Aaron sat down to pull on his shoes, and Will decided to just get it over with. Maybe if he just started talking, he'd find a way to get into something personal . . . but not *too* personal.

"So, man," Will said, sitting down next to Aaron to tie his own sneakers. "What did you do this weekend?"

Aaron shrugged one shoulder and glanced at Will, flicking back his head to get his bangs out of his eyes. "Nothing much. You?"

"Same," Will said. "Went to the beach yesterday."

"Oh, yeah?" Aaron said. He stood to pull his backpack out of his locker and ran his hands through his hair a few times. "Good beach day."

"Yeah," Will said.

Now what? he thought as Aaron slammed his locker. He wasn't even sure what it was he was supposed to be finding out about the guy. How was he going to work it into the conversation when he didn't know what it was?

"So . . . do you . . . like the beach?" he asked. *What?* What *did I just say?*

Aaron's forehead wrinkled, and he looked at Will just like he should have—like Will was suddenly speaking backward. "Yeah, I like the beach," he said. "I surf."

He surfs! Will thought. That was something he didn't know. And if he didn't know it, Cherie and Melissa probably didn't. He filed it away to tell Melissa later. Maybe Cherie could start spending more time on her board or something.

"Cool," he said. Then, just because he felt like he should say something else, he added, "I've never really gotten into it. My mom wouldn't let me."

Aaron laughed and shouldered his backpack. "You always do what your mom tells you?" he asked, his eyes mocking good-naturedly.

"No," Will said. His face burned bright red, and

he stood up and grabbed his bag. "I just meant when I was little . . . you know . . . she wouldn't let me learn."

I'm going to kill Melissa, he thought. *I can't believe she made me do this.*

"Oh," Aaron said with a nod, still grinning like Will was a total mama's boy. "So are you ready or what?"

"Yeah," Will said, shaking his head as he closed his locker. He'd had just about enough of Melissa's fact-finding mission. Guys were definitely not cut out for this kind of thing. If the girls wanted to know what kind of fast food Aaron liked, fine. His favorite sports team, no problem. What else did they need to know about a person?

"So, what're you doing now?" Aaron asked as they made their way out of the locker room. The final bell rang, and the hall instantly filled with students.

Will's stomach grumbled, and he glanced at his watch. It was going to be at least four hours until he ate dinner. "Second lunch," Will said. "You wanna go grab some pizza?"

"Sounds like a plan," Aaron answered. "I don't have practice today, and I was going to stop by the video store anyway. It's right next to Guido's."

"Video store on a Monday night?" Will asked, pushing through the double doors that led to the stairwell. He had to get a couple of books out of his locker upstairs.

"Yeah," Aaron said with a shrug. "I know it sounds lame, but my mom and I have a standing tradition on Monday nights. We rent a classic movie and get Chinese food. We've been doing it ever since I was a kid."

Will cracked up laughing as he climbed the stairs. "Who's the mama's boy now?" he asked, glancing at Aaron over his shoulder.

"Hey, don't knock a good black and white until you've tried it," Aaron said nonchalantly. Clearly Will's mocking didn't bother him nearly as much as his bothered Will. "Classic movies are cool. They really don't make them like they used to."

Will rolled his eyes as he opened the door at the top of the stairs. "Yeah, now they make them *good*," he said.

"Whatever, dude," Aaron said. "I'll meet you at your car."

They parted to go to their lockers, and Will shook his head as he loped off down the hall. Classic movies. Sheesh. If Cherie knew *that*, she probably wouldn't want to date the guy anymore. He reminded himself to tell Melissa about the surfing and then turned his mind to more important things. Now, what was he going to get on his pizza . . . ?

Elizabeth Wakefield

That story was totally about me. The more I think about it, the more sure I am. Consider the evidence.

The guitar was made of blond wood. Blonde. Get it? Plus it was the musician's first guitar, and I was Conner's first love. Yeah, he'd gone out with a lot of girls before me, but he definitely felt more strongly about me than anyone who came before.

So I'm the precious guitar. Conner is the musician. That means the new, fancy guitars the musician tried out clearly represent Alanna. So when the musician got tired of the new guitars, he went looking for the first guitar again, only to find out it was gone forever.

Think about it. Conner and Alanna just broke up, and when Conner went looking for _me_, he realized I was with Jeff — that is, gone forever!

It's so perfectly clear.

. . . So what am I going to do about it?

Ulterior Motives 5

"Hey, Liss," Will said when Melissa climbed into the passenger seat of his Blazer on Monday evening. He leaned over to give her a kiss, and she pursed her lips, giving him a quick peck.

"Hi," she said briskly, all business.

Will resisted the urge to roll his eyes. She'd called him a little bit earlier and told him she had a craving for hazelnut coffee and asked if he wanted to go to House of Java. Of course, Will wasn't stupid. He had a feeling there was an ulterior motive here.

"So . . . why the sudden urge for coffee?" he asked innocently. "Planning on pulling an all-nighter or something?"

"No," Melissa said with a quick shrug. "I just called you because I wanted to see you."

"Yeah, right," Will said, glancing at her out of the corner of his eye. That was why she'd kissed him with all the warmth of Jack Frost—because she was feeling romantic. "More like you wanted to see if I found out anything about Aaron."

Melissa flushed slightly. "Maybe," she said, fiddling with the rope that tied her sweater together at the front. "Did you?"

Will clenched his jaw as he came to a stop at a red light. "What is with you?" he asked, glancing at her out of the corner of his eye. "It's like Aaron is all you can think about lately. Why do you care so much?"

Melissa's mouth fell open. "I'm just trying to help Cherie," she said, turning her profile to him to stare through the windshield. "I saw her this afternoon, and she seemed kind of . . . you know . . . lovelorn." She tucked her hair behind her ear and looked at him again quickly. "So did you find anything out or what?"

"Who uses words like *lovelorn?*" Will asked with a chuckle.

"Will!" she blurted out, obviously getting impatient.

"Okay! Okay! As a matter of fact, I did find out something," Will said, feeling quite satisfied with himself as he hit the gas again. "Aaron is apparently a huge surfer."

"Well, duh," Melissa said, snorting a laugh. "Everyone knows that."

"What?" Will said, his face turning red. "I didn't know it." Perfect. He'd thought he'd done his job and Melissa would be psyched. Now she was probably going to make him go back and try all over again. Just what he needed. If these deep conversations kept up, Aaron was going to start to think that *Will* was interested in him.

"Is that it? That's *all* you found out?" Melissa asked, starting to get huffy. She crossed her arms over her chest and set her jaw. "I wanted you to find out what he liked in a girl, not uncover something that was total public knowledge and wouldn't help even if it wasn't!"

Will felt his blood start to boil, and he gripped the steering wheel. What was Melissa's problem anyway? It wasn't like he'd offered to help—she'd enlisted him. And wasn't there some saying about beggars not being choosers?

Melissa looked down at the floor, and then her eyebrows knotted up. "What's with the popcorn?" she asked, kicking at a bag of unpopped microwave corn he'd picked up at the video store that afternoon.

"Oh, Aaron and I dropped by Blockbuster on the way home so Aaron could rent some stupid movie," Will said, still feeling belligerent. "They were having a sale on snacks, so I—"

"Wait, Aaron rented a movie?" Melissa interrupted, sitting up straight in her seat.

"Uh . . . yeah," Will answered. "What's the big deal?"

"Which movie?" she asked.

"*Casablanca,* actually," Will said, scoffing. "Apparently he has some jones on for classic movies."

Melissa laughed and shook her head, smiling that smile she had that made Will feel like he was about two inches tall. "I can't believe you," Melissa said. "*That's* useful information. If he likes classic movies, he probably likes girls who like classic movies."

"And girls who surf," Will added, trying to make his point.

"Okay, and girls who surf," Melissa said with a huge roll of the eyes. "Unfortunately," she added under her breath.

"Why unfortunately?" Will asked, confused. "Cherie's a great surfer."

"Right," Melissa said. "I know. Okay . . . is there anything else you can think of? Anything at all?"

Racking his brain, even though he was completely sick of the subject, Will mentally went through the afternoon. They'd gone to get pizza, then to the video store. Aaron had picked out the movie quickly, and then they'd gone to the counter and—

"Yes! He thought the girl behind the counter was cute," Will said, hitting the steering wheel with the heel of his hand. "And she was definitely a tomboy type. She was wearing a little sweatshirt and had her hair back under a baseball cap. Oh! And she snorted when she laughed, and Aaron said he loved it when his ex-girlfriend used to do that."

"Really?" Melissa asked, grinning. "This is perfect!" She was practically glowing as Will pulled into a parking spot in front of HOJ.

"So," Will asked, unbuckling his seat belt. "Got enough to work with now?" He *so* wanted to be off the hook.

Melissa grinned at him. "Yeah. I think I do."

Elizabeth sat across the kitchen table from Jeff, bent over her creative-writing notebook, trying to work on her next short-short story. Or at least, that's what she hoped she *looked* like she was doing. Actually she was going over Conner's story again and again in her mind. Hearing him say, *"I wasn't sure what you'd think,"* over and over.

She couldn't stop thinking about Conner. Even though she was sitting with her perfectly wonderful, hot, intelligent, crazy-in-love-with-her boyfriend. She couldn't stop thinking about Conner, and she couldn't stop wondering if he was thinking about her too.

"What're you thinking about?" Jeff asked out of nowhere.

Elizabeth flushed and looked up at him, blinking a few times as she tried to come up with an answer.

Something other than, *"I was daydreaming about my ex. Thanks for asking."*

"What?" she said, her forehead wrinkling as she stalled for time.

"You had a kind of wicked smile on your face," he said, putting down his pen and leaning forward with a grin, his green eyes twinkling. "Care to share?"

Omigod, I'm evil, Elizabeth thought.

"Sorry. It's not that interesting," she said as she swallowed back her guilt. She pushed her blond hair behind her shoulders, shifted in her seat, and pulled her notebook closer to her. "I was just trying to decide what to write about." She raised her eyebrows hopefully, thinking it was a good time to change the subject. "Got any good ideas for a short-short story?"

Jeff leaned back in his chair and tapped his pen against the tabletop as he thought. "Let's see," he said, squinting as he stared at some random point behind Elizabeth's head.

Then, out of nowhere, he started to suck at his teeth. Actually sucked at his teeth. Elizabeth squirmed a bit while trying very hard not to look disturbed. She hated when Jeff sucked his teeth. She'd hated it last year when they were together, and she hadn't missed it when they'd broken up.

Conner would never do anything that icky, Elizabeth thought, her face screwing up with disgust.

I can't believe I just thought that, she told herself, her heart dropping. *I am not going to compare Jeff to Conner. I'm not. Jeff is perfect. And Conner is ... well ...*

"How about a story about a guy and a girl who break up for stupid reasons but then, after spending some time apart, find a way to be together again and live happily ever after?" Jeff suggested finally.

Elizabeth froze. What was he doing, reading her mind? Why would he suggest she write a story about her and Conner getting back together?

Jeff reached across the table and took one of her hands in both of his. "Of course you'd have to ... you know ... make the guy a damn handsome redhead with a killer sense of style," he joked, tucking his chin.

"Of course," Elizabeth said with a laugh. She was half relieved and half mortified. Here Jeff was trying to flirt with her, and all she could think about was Conner McDermott!

"So? What do you think?" Jeff said, letting go of her hand and sitting back in his chair. "They do say to write what you know."

"Yeah ...," Elizabeth said, chewing on the end of her pen as she mulled it over. She was pretty sure she didn't want to write a romance, though. It was so predictable—pensive teenage girls writing about teenage love. She wanted to write something ... deeper.

"I don't know. I don't really feel up to doing this

right now." She shut her notebook and sighed, suddenly feeling extremely tired.

"Okay. Do you want to go grab some dinner?" Jeff said, picking his bag up off the chair at the end of the table. He started to shove a few books into his bag. "There's a new Japanese place downtown, and I—"

"Do you mind if I skip it?" Elizabeth asked. Suddenly she felt like being alone. Or at least away from Jeff. All this being with him and thinking about Conner was making her tense. And since she couldn't seem to control her mind . . .

"Really? I thought that was the plan. Study, then dinner," Jeff said, his lightly freckled face falling.

"Yeah, but I didn't exactly get much studying done. And I have a lot to do tonight," Elizabeth said apologetically. She couldn't believe she was doing this. Jeff was so obviously disappointed, and why? So that she could sit here and daydream about another guy all night. A guy that had broken her heart on more than one occasion. What was wrong with her?

Jeff finished organizing his things and stood. "Okay," he said. "I understand. Sometimes I concentrate better when I'm alone too."

Elizabeth stood and wrapped her arms around Jeff's neck, her heart feeling heavy with guilt. "Thanks for being so cool about this," she said.

"I *know* I can't concentrate when I'm around

74

you," Jeff said with a grin. He leaned forward and touched his lips to Elizabeth's. She kissed him back but broke it off quickly. She was feeling too confused and guilty to get into kissing him.

"Well, I guess I'll see you tomorrow," Jeff said as he turned to go.

Elizabeth followed him, shoving her hands in the back pockets of her jeans. *At least he hasn't noticed anything's wrong,* she thought with a sigh. *Nothing is wrong!* she reminded herself. *Everything is perfect with Jeff!*

Elizabeth brought her hand to her head as Jeff opened the door. She was starting to get a bit of a headache from all these warring thoughts. Maybe she could exorcise herself of this Conner thing tonight, and by the time she saw Jeff again, she'd be back to her normal, levelheaded self.

"Are you okay?" Jeff asked, pausing on the front step.

"Yeah. Just thinking about stuff," Elizabeth said, tucking her hair behind her ears.

"Okay, well, call me if you need any more help," Jeff said. Then, with another quick kiss, he headed off toward his car.

Elizabeth closed the door and then leaned back against it, squeezing her eyes shut. Why was Conner in her head again? And how could she be insane enough to let it get in between her and Jeff?

*　　*　　*

Within seconds of Jeremy pushing the Wakefield doorbell on Monday night, Elizabeth swung open the door, scaring him nearly out of his skin. It also didn't do much good for his still fragile stomach.

"Hey, Liz," he said, catching his breath as his heart rate started to slow down. "Were you waiting for someone?"

"No. Just said good-bye to Jeff, actually," Elizabeth said with a weak smile. "Sorry if I scared you."

She stepped aside so that he could come in, and he lifted the shopping bag he'd brought. "Saltines and seltzer," he told her. "I thought I'd treat my girl to the best."

"Yeah, that's pretty much all she's been eating," Elizabeth said. "She's in the den, watching TV."

"Thanks," Jeremy said. He glanced at her as he started across the living room. "Are you going to join us?" he asked.

"No, thanks," Elizabeth said. "I've got a lot of work."

"Okay."

Jeremy could hear the laugh track on the sitcom Jessica was watching as he made his way around the couch. He was actually kind of glad Elizabeth had turned down his offer. He liked Jessica's sister well enough, but he hadn't seen Jessica since Friday, and it felt more like a month apart than a few days.

"Hey, beautiful," he said, sliding open the door. She

was sprawled out on the couch in gray sweats, a beat-up SVU sweatshirt, and a pair of huge white socks.

"You look like crap," she said with a smirk.

"You too," he shot back. "I was just being charitable."

"Ha ha," Jessica said, sitting up and tightening the ponytail that sat almost directly on top of her head.

Jeremy placed his bag on the coffee table, sat down next to her, and planted a kiss on her forehead. She actually did look beautiful. Pale and sickly, but still beautiful. It was kind of amazing, actually. Jessica leaned forward and pulled the box of crackers out of the bag.

"Saltines! My favorite!" she said, batting her eyelashes at him.

"Hey, I do what I can," Jeremy said, putting his arm around her shoulders. Jessica settled into the crook between his arm and his chest and nestled closer to him. Jeremy smiled. Yep. Sick or not, this was the life.

"So . . . did you talk to Ally today?" she asked.

"No," Jeremy said with a sigh. "I wouldn't be surprised if she never wanted to speak to us again."

"Yeah. She pretty much went ballistic," Jessica said, placing her hand on Jeremy's chest.

"Trust me, I know. Why did she have to be so annoying about it?" Jeremy said, slouching down a little farther and bringing Jessica with him. "She wouldn't even let me explain what happened."

"Yeah, but you know how HOJ is on Sundays," Jessica said, glancing up at him with her big blue-green eyes. "She was expecting her two best people, and we both called out. I'm sure she got slammed, and I bet Corey wasn't any help. I probably would have freaked too."

Jeremy closed his eyes and tipped back his head. "Yeah, you're right," he said. Ally did have a good reason to be angry. But she had to let him explain what happened. He hated the idea that she thought he and Jessica were trying to take advantage of her. It kind of offended him, actually. She should know them better than that by now. They'd never both call out on the same day . . . at least not on a Sunday.

"So, are you working tomorrow?" he asked, kissing the top of Jessica's head.

"Nope," she said. "Why?"

"Because I am," he explained. "And I *really* don't want to face the beast alone."

"You'll be fine," Jessica said, whacking him on the chest. "And don't call her a beast."

"Okay!" Jeremy said, his stomach twisting. "Just don't hit me again. Who knows what could happen?"

Jessica looked up at him, all concerned. "Oh! Sorry!" she said. "Are you okay?"

Jeremy smiled and touched his nose to hers. She

was so incredibly sweet and perfect, sometimes he just couldn't handle it.

"I'm fine," he said, touching his lips to hers. "You know, we'd better make the most of this night. After Ally gets done with me . . ."

"You're right," Jessica said with a conspiratorial grin. "This could be the last time I ever see you."

She cuddled closer to him and kissed him again, slipping her hand around his neck. Jeremy kissed her back, feeling better than he had in days. In moments he forgot all about his stomach and about Ally.

It really was unbelievable the effect Jessica had on him.

Conner McDermott

The phone is sitting there, mocking me. It's mocking me because it knows I want to call her. But I won't. Not anymore. I do have pride, you know. I do have a backbone.

And it's time I started using it.

So I'm not going to call her. I won't. Even if I can't stop thinking about her. I may not have control over my brain, but I do have control over my fingers.

That's something.

Kind of.

CHAPTER
The Wrath of Ally
6

Elizabeth emerged from the lunch line on Tuesday afternoon and started toward the table she usually shared with Jessica, Tia, Andy, Ken, and Maria. As she was making her way down the center aisle between tables, she happened to catch a glimpse of a well-worn brown suede jacket, and she slowed down, trying not to look like she was looking. Conner and Tia were sitting at the end of a table against the wall, and they seemed to be involved in a not too heavy conversation.

I can't . . . can I? Elizabeth thought, realizing she had about two seconds to decide before she started sticking out like a sore, lost thumb.

She cast a glance over her shoulder to Jeff's table. He was laughing it up with a few of the guys from the soccer team and hadn't noticed her standing there. Without giving herself time to get nervous, Elizabeth turned and made a beeline for Tia and Conner.

"Hey, guys," she said when she got to the end of their table.

They both looked up. Tia's eyes were wide and a bit . . . well . . . baffled. Conner's were surprised, but he quickly covered that, of course.

Elizabeth's heart squeezed in her chest, but she wouldn't let herself back away now. Clutching her tray, she gestured at one of the empty chairs with her elbow. "Can I sit, or are you guys . . . ?"

Tia looked at Conner, who simply looked back, his expression completely blank. "Yeah," Tia said, her eyes never leaving Conner's face. She was obviously trying to figure out what had drawn Elizabeth to their table. "Sit."

Sliding behind Tia's back, Elizabeth put down her tray and then dropped into the chair next to her friend's. Her pulse was racing, and she wondered if she looked as nervous as she felt. Conner's eyes flicked up and met hers.

"Hey," she said. Her face flushed, but she chose to ignore it. It was hot in here, that was all.

"Hey," he said back.

"Okay. What's going on here?" Tia asked, folding her arms on the table and shaking her wavy hair behind her shoulders. "What's with all the civility?"

Elizabeth smiled and shrugged one shoulder.

"Since when are we not civil?" she said, looking at Conner out of the corner of her eye.

"We are nothing if not civil," Conner agreed.

Tia took a deep breath and rolled her eyes, obviously skeptical. "Oookay," she said. "I'm down with the alternate-universe thing."

Conner chuckled and tossed a french fry into his mouth. Elizabeth felt her heart warm. It was really nice to see Conner laugh again. It was, in fact, nice to see Conner looking something other than totally depressed. And she was glad to be a part of his nondepression.

"So, were you guys talking about anything important?" Elizabeth asked as she twisted the top off her water bottle. "Because I could use some help on something."

"Shoot!" Tia said, leaning back in her chair and pulling her hooded sweatshirt closer around her body. "I'm all ears."

"Well, I'm having trouble with a creative-writing assignment," Elizabeth explained. She took a sip of her water and leaned her cheek on her hand. "I can't figure out what to write about."

"This sounds like something for Mr. McDermott," Tia said, smiling across the table at Conner. "And since we *are* functioning in this alternate universe, I'm *sure* he'd be willing to help."

Elizabeth's blush deepened, and she looked down

83

at her food. "Okay, Tia, you're having a little bit too much fun with this," she said. Still, maybe Conner would take Tia up on it. How great would it be to get his help on her assignment? And it just might lead to a conversation about the subject of *his* last piece.

"So? What do you think, Not-so-stoic Boy?" Tia asked, arching one eyebrow. "Ya gonna help her or what?"

Conner let out an audible sigh and then sat silent for a couple of seconds. Elizabeth felt her shoulders tense up. He was going to turn her down. How mortifying! Why had she come over here? And why did Tia have to offer up his services?

"Yeah, I guess," he said finally, picking at the rim on his tray. "Whatever."

Not exactly an enthusiastic response.

"You don't have to," Elizabeth said, clutching her hands together under the table and feeling like a total moron. "I'm sure it'll be fine."

"No. I want to," Conner said, pushing himself up in his seat. He looked Elizabeth in the eye. "We're friends, right? Friends can help friends with homework."

Elizabeth grinned, her shoulders instantly relaxing again. "Yeah. Friends can help friends," she said. She couldn't have stopped smiling if she'd tried. He'd called them friends! How great was that? "How's tomorrow after school?" she asked. "I'm off from work. We can go to House of Java or something."

"Yeah. Sounds good," Conner said with a nod, then he returned his full attention to his french fries.

Elizabeth picked up her sandwich to take a bite, but Tia discreetly touched her thigh before she could.

"What's the deal?" Tia mouthed, motioning to Conner with her eyes.

"No deal," Elizabeth mouthed back, still grinning. *"We're just friends."*

"Yeah, right," Tia mouthed. She rolled her eyes and then went back to her lunch.

Elizabeth took a bite of her sandwich, but she was almost too giddy to eat. Tia knew Conner better than anyone. If she thought something was up, then something was probably up. Now all Elizabeth had to do was figure out whether or not she *wanted* something to be up.

"I don't believe this," Alanna said, glaring at her reflection in the mirror above her dresser.

She'd put on a tank top and shorts so that she could inspect as much of her body as possible, and what she saw was not pretty. Her skin was still ruddy and uneven after her bout with hives on Sunday afternoon. She'd stayed home from school for two days, and she was about to die from boredom. Still, it was a better fate than showing up in homeroom looking like a freak show.

"At least it's not like anyone interesting is going to pop by," Alanna said, looking down at her splotchy arm as her mind flashed on an image of Conner. He probably would have died laughing if he'd seen her like this. Either that or run in the other direction.

But it didn't matter. Because there was no way he was going to randomly stop by.

Conner had done his share of surprise appearances in the past, but that was clearly over. If he was going to come over and apologize to her, he would have done it by now. Obviously she didn't mean enough to him anymore to merit the use of gas. He'd even stopped calling. Not that she cared. She was done with him too.

Still, it did kind of sting.

"Alanna? Can I come in?" her mother called from outside the door.

"Yeah," Alanna called back. She turned and walked over to her bed, sitting down to face the door. As her mother peeked her head into the room, Alanna pulled her throw pillow onto her lap.

"How are you?" her mother asked, wincing the moment she saw Alanna's skin.

"Still red," Alanna answered, toying with the

pillow fringe as always. It was amazing the thing still had any fringe left to toy with. Especially now that these motherly visits to her room were becoming more and more frequent. "Too bad we don't live in Colorado. I could get away with leaving the house if I could wear a turtleneck."

Her mother smiled at her joke, then slid into the room along the wall as if Alanna had cooties. Or, possibly, she was concerned that Alanna was going to attack in seek of retribution.

"Listen, I'm really sorry about what happened," Mrs. Feldman said once again. "All I wanted was for us to have some time together."

"It's okay, Mom," Alanna said, concentrating on the fringe. Of course, if that was really all her mother wanted, she should have asked Alanna what she'd wanted to do. They could have compromised. But instead she'd dragged her to a bunch of stupid places Alanna would never have set foot in otherwise. Including the hospital.

At this point she was starting to feel that hanging out with her mother was too dangerous for her own good.

"Well, I think I've found a way to make it up to you," her mother said with a smile. She pulled two tickets out from behind her back and waved them in the air.

Oh, no, Alanna thought, squinting at the tiny pieces of paper. *This can't be good.*

"I got us two tickets to the Boy Toy concert this Friday night!" Her mother gave a little jump, and Alanna was struck with a sudden, disturbing image of her mother as a cheerleader.

"Boy Toy?" Alanna said, trying ever so hard not to sound as disgusted as she felt. Was her mother on drugs? Did Alanna *look* like the kind of person who would be into a boy band? Did she look like the kind of person who would be into a bunch of guys who didn't even play their own instruments . . . probably didn't actually sing their own songs? If you could even call them that.

"Well? Aren't you excited?" her mother asked, taking a step farther into her room.

"Yeah. That's great," Alanna said flatly.

What was with her parents? When they'd first gotten back from Chicago, they'd told her they were going to change—that they wanted to hear about what was bothering her and what was going on in her life. And for a little while Alanna had actually let herself believe them. But now it was abundantly clear that her parents were just as clueless as she'd always thought they were. Neither of them had tried to talk to her about anything serious. Her father was as nonexistent as he'd always been, and all her mother seemed to want to do was drag her along to all of these silly activities and make her into the daughter she *wished* she had.

"I'm really looking forward to this, Alanna," her mother said, placing the tickets on top of her dresser.

I'd rather get another avocado mud bath, Alanna thought. And for a moment she thought about saying it, but she just couldn't hurt her mother's feelings. The woman was obviously upset about Sunday's mistakes. Alanna didn't want to rub it in her face that she'd made another one.

"Me too," she said finally, leaning back into her pillows as she imagined an arena full of screaming girls carrying I Love Boy Toy posters and crying every time the guys onstage moved their hips. Suddenly she felt extraordinarily tired.

"I think I'm going to try to take a nap, okay?" Alanna said, letting out a huge yawn for effect.

"Sure," her mother said. "Feel better, honey." She backed out of the room and closed the door with a click. Once again Alanna was left alone.

She took a deep breath and stared up at the ceiling, her chest feeling heavy and tight. She'd never spent so much time with her mother, but somehow she'd also never felt so lonely. Suddenly she missed Conner more than she could bear. She wished he'd never come into her life in the first place because now that she knew what it was like to have someone like that—someone who knew her so well and cared so much about her—she missed it more than she could have imagined.

When Jeremy walked into House of Java on Tuesday evening, he felt like he was arriving for his first shift ever. He was so nervous, he had to concentrate in order to swallow. The place was fairly quiet—just a few people scattered at different tables and no one on line. Jeremy walked behind the counter and slid past Corey, who was leaning into the counter, popping her bubble gum over some random 'zine.

"You sure you want to go back there?" she asked without looking up.

Jeremy glanced at the back of her dyed black hair, which she had divided into three ponytails. "That bad, huh?" he asked.

"Ever see *The Exorcist*?" she asked without a shred of irony.

Great, Jeremy thought. *This is going to be fun.*

He paused outside the doors to the back room, took a deep breath, then pushed his way through. There was no point in postponing the inevitable. And the wrath of Ally was obviously inevitable.

She was sitting at her desk near the door, and Jeremy froze in his tracks, waiting for her to attack. She looked up from her paperwork, her pen poised over an invoice, and smiled. Okay, that was unexpected. But at least it was a good sign. At least she was giving him time to apologize before she laced into him.

"Listen, Ally, I'm really sorry about—"

"Please. It's okay," Ally said, raising one hand dismissively. "What you did on Sunday was really great."

Jeremy's mouth was still hanging open midsentence, and he couldn't seem to get it to close. He looked over his shoulder to see if anyone was filming him. This had to be a joke. What was she talking about?

"Um . . . are you okay?" he asked her, holding his hand out in front of him. "Did you hit your head this morning or something?"

"Uh . . . no," Ally said with a laugh as she copied numbers from one column to another. "I just think you owe your friend Trent a big thank-you. He's a hard worker, and he did a great job."

Jeremy's brow knitted, and he looked at the ground, trying to make any kind of sense of this conversation. As far as he knew, Ally didn't even *know* Trent. And he couldn't think of a single reason he'd owe Trent a thank-you.

"Okay, *what* are you talking about?" Jeremy asked. "Was Trent here or something?"

Ally turned in her chair and crossed her legs, looking up at Jeremy with confusion. "Yeah, he was here. Didn't you ask him to come in for you?"

"No," Jeremy said, feeling like he was dreaming. This was so out of nowhere. "I had no idea."

"Well, then you owe him an even bigger thank-you," Ally said, turning back to her work. "I would never volunteer to come work here and then not even take credit for it."

For a moment Jeremy just stood there, trying to figure out what had transpired. Trent had come in to work his shift? How was that even possible? Trent had never worked a day before in his life. And why? Why would he do it?

"Um . . . Jeremy? I do need you to work tonight, eventually," Ally said, eyeing him like he was dangerous.

"Right. Sorry," Jeremy said, snapping back into the now.

He ran a hand over his dark hair and slowly walked over to the shelves where the staff kept all their stuff. Absently tossing his backpack up next to Corey's bag, Jeremy turned over this new development in his mind, but it was so totally bizarre, he didn't even know how to process it. What had Trent been thinking, coming in to work for him? Did he think he was going to get somewhere doing Jeremy a secret favor? He took one of the many green aprons down from a hook and tied it on, then went back out into the café.

None of this made any sense to him, but one thing was certain—he was going to have to talk to Trent.

Alanna Feldman

I put the phone in the closet. I had to. It was mocking me. I swear it was. Every single time I looked at it, I could hear it teasing me. <u>"You wanna call him! You wanna call him!"</u>

But I don't. I do not. Still, I had to get the phone out of my face. It was the only way I could make myself stop thinking about him.

But I guess I haven't really stopped thinking about him, huh?

Damn.

CHAPTER 7

Endless Stalemate

Trent sat at the breakfast table on Wednesday morning, munching on a well-toasted English muffin and watching some mindless cartoon on the mini-TV. His eyes were only half open, even though he'd been awake for half an hour. Morning was not Trent's time of day. But the moment he heard Jeremy coming down the stairs, an adrenaline rush shook his body awake. Trent never knew when Jeremy might break the stalemate and be ready to talk things out.

And if this wasn't that time, the silent treatment he always got from his former best friend was usually enough to put him on edge.

Jeremy's sneakers squeaked against the floor as he stopped in the kitchen doorway. He glanced at Trent, his eyes betraying nothing—except for the fact that he was much more awake than Trent was.

"Hey, man," Jeremy said as he dropped his backpack on one of the chairs around the table and walked over to the refrigerator.

That was something, at least. Trent couldn't remember the last time Jeremy had greeted him first. It was like he was always hoping there was a chance he wouldn't have to talk to Trent at all.

"Hey. How's it going?" Trent said, wiping melted butter off his hands with his napkin.

"Fine." Jeremy walked over to the table, twisting open a bottle of Snapple. He stood across from Trent and took a sip, looking Trent up and down as if he was wondering whether or not to say something.

"Listen, that was really cool . . . what you did on Sunday," Jeremy said finally. "Thanks. Because of you, I think, Ally didn't fire me."

Trent felt a welcome and long overdue wave of relief wash through his body. "You're welcome. It was really no problem," he said with a grin.

"But you should know, this doesn't just make what you did okay," Jeremy continued, his jaw clenching.

The smile fell right off Trent's face. "Look, Jeremy, I—"

"I'm sorry, Trent, but you broke the cardinal rule," Jeremy said firmly. "You don't go after your best friend's girlfriend. You just don't."

Trent racked his brain for something to say but came up blank. There was nothing he *could* say. Jeremy was right. He had completely betrayed their friendship. He was sure that if Jeremy had done the same thing to him, it would take him a long time to get over it. The question was, how long?

"I understand," Trent managed to say, looking down at the table. He was suddenly sick to his stomach, and all he wanted was to end this conversation as quickly as possible.

"Good," Jeremy said. He picked up his bag and slung it over his shoulder, then turned and walked out of the house without another word.

Trent didn't move a muscle until he heard Jeremy's car peel out of the driveway, and then he let out a long breath and slumped back in his chair. Yes, he understood why Jeremy was mad at him, but this endless stalemate was a little hard to swallow. They had both moved on with their lives. Jeremy and Jessica were together and perfectly happy, and Trent was back with Tia now. It wasn't like Trent was even remotely interested in Jessica anymore. He wasn't even sure he ever *had* been. He'd long since chalked up the attraction to temporary insanity.

So when was it going to end? When were they all going to be friends again?

Elizabeth glanced at her silver watch as she rushed through the halls late on Wednesday morning. For some reason, she'd been checking the time every two minutes all day long. It wasn't like she had someplace to be. She was stuck in school until two forty-five no matter what, so who cared what time it was?

You do, the little voice in her mind teased as she stopped in front of her locker. *You want the day to end because you're hanging out with Conner after school today.*

A little skitter of excitement tingled over her skin, and she had to stop herself from smiling. She was not allowed to be excited about this. It was a study session. Nothing more.

And besides, you're with Jeff now, she reminded herself as she spun her lock. *Jeff, Jeff, Jeff, Jeff, Jeff.*

"Hey, Liz!"

Her hand flew up to cover her heart, and she looked up to find Jeff himself standing right next to her, a lazy grin on his face as he leaned his shoulder against the next locker. Her heart flopped in her chest at the sight of him, and she realized she must be losing it. Excited over Conner, excited over Jeff . . . why did her life seem to get more complicated each day?

"Hi," she said, finally catching her breath. "Sorry, you scared me."

"Yeah. You looked like you were off in la-la land," Jeff said as she pulled a few books out of her locker. "Daydreaming about me again?"

Elizabeth laughed as her face flushed red. It was a

really good thing that people couldn't read each other's minds.

"I'll take that as a yes," Jeff joked, putting his hands in the pockets of his well-worn chinos.

"You do that," Elizabeth said flirtatiously.

What am I doing? she chided herself. *I'm so evil!*

"Hey, I heard that Michelle Mann is doing a book signing at Bookends downtown tonight," Jeff said, pushing himself away from the wall to stand up straight. "Wanna go?"

"You're kidding me," Elizabeth said, her jaw dropping. She couldn't believe it. Michelle Mann wasn't only an amazing novelist, but she was also the main reason Elizabeth wanted to get into writing in the first place. "I *love* Michelle Mann."

"I know. You only have like ten of her books on the shelves in your room," Jeff said with a grin.

"Wow. You're observant," Elizabeth said, another painful pang of guilt driving through her heart. Jeff was such a great guy. He paid attention, he knew what she liked, he wanted to take her to this signing even though he probably couldn't care less about Michelle Mann. And she was going to have to say no.

"Should I pick you up? She's going to start at six, so I figure if we get there at five-thirty, we'll be good," Jeff said, obviously figuring there was no way Elizabeth could turn down this opportunity.

She thought about it for a moment, realizing this was probably her only chance to meet one of her biggest heroes. But then she thought of Conner. And about how psyched she'd been when he offered to help her. And about the fact that she'd been looking forward to it all day. And somehow those thoughts shoved Michelle Mann right out of her mind.

"I . . . can't make it," Elizabeth said slowly, returning her attention to her locker in an attempt to avoid eye contact. If she looked at Jeff, he'd know something was up.

"You're kidding," Jeff said. "I thought you'd be psyched. And I know you don't have to work."

Elizabeth just kept shuffling around in her locker, stalling. What was she supposed to say? *"I'm going to miss this once-in-a-lifetime chance because I want to flirt with my ex-boyfriend"*? No. *"Because I want to get help with my creative-writing assignment from my ex-boyfriend"*? Not a good idea either, considering she'd already shot down Jeff's idea for her piece. Now what?

"I . . . well . . ."

Suddenly Elizabeth decided the only way out was a half-truth. That way she would be clear to see Conner, but Jeff wouldn't get hurt . . . hopefully.

"You're probably not going to like this," Elizabeth said, looking up at him through her lashes.

"What?" Jeff said, his face falling slightly. "Is something wrong?"

"No. Not at all," Elizabeth said, closing her locker and leaning back against it, clutching a few books to her chest. "It's just I'm supposed to see Conner this afternoon."

Jeff's tan, freckled face suddenly went impossibly pale. "Oh," he said, his brow furrowed.

"It's just . . . he broke up with his girlfriend, and he's really upset about it and he needs all the friends he can get right now," Elizabeth explained quickly, clueless as to whether or not she sounded convincing. "I promised him we'd do something this afternoon."

"What kind of thing are you thinking about doing?" Jeff asked point-blank.

"We're just gonna get some coffee and study," Elizabeth explained, looking Jeff in the eye. "As *friends*." *Supposedly,* she added mentally.

"As friends," Jeff repeated. The color started to return to his cheeks. "You're sure."

"Yes, I'm sure," Elizabeth said, feeling like a total jerk. She wasn't exactly lying to Jeff. As far as she knew, right now she and Conner were just friends. And she wasn't sure either of them wanted anything more.

Then why do you feel so guilty? she asked herself as she and Jeff started off toward class.

"Okay, I understand," Jeff said, dragging his feet slightly. "Hey! Maybe I'll go and get you her autograph."

Elizabeth smiled even as her stomach turned. "That would be great," she said. She stopped and squeezed his arm so that he would stop too. Then she stood on her toes and kissed him. "You're the best," she said, looking into his smiling green eyes.

And he was. Unfortunately, at that moment, she couldn't help thinking that she didn't deserve him.

"I think we can wrap it up early," Melissa told Aaron on Wednesday afternoon, pushing up the sleeves of her SVH sweatshirt. "After all, it *is* your birthday."

Aaron grinned at her from across the table and slapped his Shakespeare book closed. "I was hoping you'd say that," he told her. "Not that I don't enjoy our little study sessions . . ."

"You do?" Melissa asked with a slow smile.

"Sure." Aaron leaned back in his chair and shrugged. "They're just not birthday worthy, ya know?"

"I can see that," Melissa said.

She gathered up her books and slid them into her bag with a half-happy, half-tired sigh. She and Aaron had gone over the themes in *Julius Caesar,* and her brain was a little fried, but even in her exhausted state, she could tell he was flirting with her. Apparently the whole tomboy thing really did work for him. She should wear her hair in a ponytail more often. Of course, Will would think she was starting to lose it.

"Seriously, though, I really want to thank you," Aaron said, flicking his bangs off his face. "I really feel like I'm getting somewhere with this stuff."

"Oh, it's no problem," Melissa said, actually feeling gratified that Aaron was learning something. When she'd decided to do this tutoring gig, she'd never really thought about the tutoring part—only the getting-back-at-Cherie-and-Will part. As a matter of fact . . .

"So, how was your big date with Cherie yesterday?" she asked, leaning her elbow on the table and propping her chin on her hand.

Aaron blushed a deep red and glanced away for a split second, apparently surprised by the question. "I didn't know it was a *big date*," he said, grabbing his pen. He popped the capped end into his mouth and started to gnaw. "Cherie told you about it?"

"Yeah," Melissa said innocently. "She seemed pretty psyched."

"Oh, yeah?" Aaron said. Melissa was disappointed to see that Aaron seemed intrigued by this news.

Apparently she'd gone one bit of information too far. "Well, we had a good time. At least I know I did."

"That's great," Melissa said, forcing enthusiasm. Then she went in for the kill. "Did she get you a present?"

Aaron shifted in his seat and leaned into the table himself. "Don't tell her, okay? But that was kind of the low point."

Melissa scrunched up her face in sympathy. "Really?" she asked. "It wasn't good?"

"It was *all right*," Aaron said, fiddling with the edge of his notebook. "It was a classic-rock CD. I guess I'm just not into it."

"That's too bad," Melissa said, reaching into her bag. It was all she could do to keep from laughing with giddiness, both over Cherie's botched gift and what she was about to do. "I'm sure she put a lot of thought into it."

She casually pulled out her Discman and popped it open. Aaron, of course, looked over, curious to see what she was listening to. His face lit up, and he lifted his eyes to hers, obviously impressed.

"That's the new Renny D.!" he said with a grin. "I've been dying to get that."

"Really?" she asked, taking out the CD. "I can burn one for you if you want."

"You're kidding! That would be great!" Aaron

said. He looked like a little boy who'd just been given his first bike.

"It's no problem," Melissa said, standing as she put her CD player back in her bag. She held on to the Renny D. CD as if she was going to be playing it in her car on the way home. In truth she'd rather be forced to eat bugs. She'd taken the disc for a test spin the night before and had turned it off within thirty seconds, vowing never to assault her eardrums with it again.

"So . . . what are you doing for your birthday?" Melissa asked as Aaron walked her to the front door.

"Ah . . . you know . . . dinner with the family," Aaron said, opening the door for her. "What are you up to?"

Melissa grinned. She couldn't have scripted this conversation more perfectly herself. "Oh, well, I don't have much homework, so I was thinking about renting a movie. I'll probably get *Philadelphia Story* or *Rear Window.*"

"You're kidding," Aaron said, his brow knitting even as he smiled. He reached up and clutched the top of the door with his hand. "*Rear Window* is one of my favorite movies of all time!"

I am so good! Melissa thought triumphantly. "Mine too," she said. "I think it's Hitchcock's best."

"Absolutely," Aaron said with a nod. "Well, enjoy."

As Melissa said good-bye, she couldn't help noticing there was a new respect in Aaron's eyes, and she felt her heart skip a beat. She was definitely getting somewhere. And it was all thanks to Will.

Could this little victory be any sweeter?

"You should give the girl some kind of fundamental weakness," Conner said, pulling his chair around the table so that it was right up against Elizabeth's. He took a sip of his coffee as he leaned over her notebook, looking over the sketchy outline for her new story.

Conner's arm brushed up against hers, and Elizabeth blushed at his closeness but tried to keep her attention on what he was saying. "You *would* think that," she said, scoffing as she tapped her pen nervously against the table. "All girls have to have a weakness."

"Whatever," Conner said, rolling his eyes. "Think about it. It would make the ending a lot stronger."

Elizabeth glanced over the notes and realized Conner was probably right. There wasn't much of a buildup before the climax of the story. If her heroine had something to overcome, her revelation at the end would have a serious emotional impact.

"What kind of weakness?" Elizabeth asked, turning her head to look Conner in the eye. When she did, her mouth was just inches from his, and her heart responded with a thump. Conner quickly leaned back in his chair, and Elizabeth couldn't help thinking he'd felt it too. That electricity.

"Alcoholism?" Conner said, staring straight ahead as she took another slug of coffee. "Just a suggestion."

Elizabeth blinked, and the pen finally ceased its maniacal tapping. Suddenly she felt intensely uncomfortable. Was he serious? Did he really want her to use his illness in her story?

"Oh ... well ... I ..."

"Don't get all freaked, Liz," he said with a smirk, wrapping both hands around his cup. "You take everything so seriously."

"I know," Elizabeth said, blushing again. She jotted the idea down in her notes, trying to think of some witty comeback. "And thanks to you, I do have some experience with it."

Conner laughed. As much as Conner ever laughed—more like a brief chuckle. But whatever it was, it made Elizabeth grin uncontrollably. She was bantering with Conner. Joking and bantering and having a good time. It was so nice. And different. He had to feel it too. If they'd been able to talk like this when they were together ... well ... things would have been a lot better.

"So, do you think you have enough to go on?" Conner asked.

"Yeah, I think so," Elizabeth responded. She flipped through her notebook and realized she had created a few pages of scrawl during their brainstorming session. "Thanks a lot, Conner, this has definitely helped."

"Huh," Conner said, gazing into his coffee.

"What?" Elizabeth asked, her brows knitting together.

"Nothing," he said, shifting in his seat and leaning into the table. "It's just nice to know somebody appreciates my help."

"Oh," Elizabeth said, closing her notebook with a smile. "Well . . . I do. This story would have reeked without your input. Now at least it has a chance."

"Why do you do that?" Conner asked, glancing up at her.

Elizabeth paused as she packed up her stuff. "Do what?" she asked as she leaned over to the floor to pick up her bag. She flipped her hair over her shoulder and tilted her head so she could see him while she groped for her backpack.

"Put yourself down all the time," Conner said. "Why do girls always do that?"

Flustered, Elizabeth had no idea how to respond. She sat up again, forgetting about the bag, and crossed her arms over her chest as she fumbled for an answer. "I don't know, I—"

"Because you shouldn't," Conner said firmly. "You're good at this, you know. You're a good . . . writer."

Elizabeth was so overwhelmed, she felt like she was going to burst. Was Conner McDermott actually sitting here complimenting her? Unbelievable. She'd never known him to waste words on being nice before. Especially not to her.

"Thanks," she said finally, realizing it was her turn to speak. Her face was so flushed, she was sure she looked like she'd been badly sunburned.

Conner blinked and looked down as if he'd just been snapped back from somewhere else.

He's definitely feeling something, Elizabeth thought. *I know he is.*

"I should go," Conner said, standing abruptly.

"Okay," Elizabeth said. "Hey, would you . . . I mean . . . could you look this over when I'm done writing it?" she asked.

Conner glanced at her papers and shrugged. "Yeah, sure. How about Friday after school?"

Elizabeth smiled. He was suggesting a time to get together. Making an actual plan. "Sounds good," she said.

"Okay. Later," Conner said.

As he made his way out of the café, Elizabeth sat back in her chair and tried to make sense of everything that had just happened. Conner had helped her, laughed with her, told her he respected her talent, and basically scolded her for being down on herself. This was not normal behavior for Stoic Boy. There had to be something behind it. There just had to be.

Conner McDermott

I can't get over how easy it is to talk to Elizabeth now that I'm not obsessed with her. I can sit across the table from her, stare into her eyes as she talks, and feel nothing.

Somehow I can't imagine ever being that way with Alanna.

Melissa Fox

Okay, don't think I'm a loser, but these classic movies aren't half bad. I rented some of them just so that I'd have something to talk about with Aaron (because we are <u>not</u> going to be able to discuss rap), and I actually think I'm going to rent a few more. The women are all beautiful, with killer clothes and perfect lives. They're all strong and interesting, and they all have men who worship them. No matter what the situation, the women always come out on top and looking just perfect through those fuzzy, grainy lenses.

But superficiality aside, I actually enjoyed watching these

movies. They have strong stories, happy endings, and a . . . I don't know . . . a positive outlook, I guess. I could use some of that in my life at the moment.

CHAPTER
Vintage Conner

8

"Let's get a table by ourselves today," Jeff suggested as he and Elizabeth paid for their lunches and joined the chaos in the cafeteria Thursday afternoon. "I feel like I haven't had a chance to talk to you in days."

That's because you haven't, Elizabeth thought, smiling at him through her guilt. She'd definitely been neglecting Jeff both in their daily life and in her mind. All her warm-and-fuzzy Jeff thoughts had seemed to be replaced by confused-and-excited Conner thoughts lately.

"Sounds good," Elizabeth said, glancing around the crowded room. "There's one over by the windows."

As they settled into chairs across from each other, Elizabeth's heart was pounding. What if Jeff asked her about what she and Conner had done the day before? He would have to be of the rare, non-jealous boyfriend variety if he didn't. What was she going to say?

That you didn't do anything interesting, she reminded herself. *Because you didn't.*

"I've got something for you," Jeff said, his eyes bright as he unzipped his bag. He pulled out a hardcover copy of Michelle Mann's latest book and opened it to the title page. Written across it in bold lettering were the words *For Elizabeth. Sorry to miss you! Good luck with your writing. —Michelle Mann.*

Elizabeth's stomach flopped as she took the book from Jeff gingerly. She couldn't believe he'd actually gone to the signing for her.

"This is unbelievable," she said. "Thank you so much. You didn't have to do that."

"Ah, it was no big deal," Jeff said as he placed his bag on the floor. "I only waited for half an hour."

"Really?" Elizabeth asked, touched. Why did Jeff have to be such a perfect boyfriend? "Thank you, really. I love it."

She stood up halfway out of her seat and leaned across the table to give him a quick kiss, but even while she was doing it, she wondered if Conner was watching. And if he was, what was he thinking? Was he jealous? Was he hurt? By the time she sat back down again, Elizabeth was blushing for the millionth time this week and feeling like a complete jerk.

"So," Jeff said, stirring his pasta around with his fork. "What did you and Conner end up doing yesterday?"

"Oh, we just got coffee and studied a little," Elizabeth said quickly. She laid her backpack on the table and placed the book carefully on top of it so that it wouldn't get messy.

"Yeah? How's he doing?" Jeff asked.

"Uh . . . fine," Elizabeth said, taken off guard. Jeff sounded like he actually cared. He didn't sound jealous or insecure but interested. "Why do you ask?"

Jeff shrugged, taking a bite of his lunch. "I don't know—I guess I feel bad for the guy. Breakups suck," he said. "And honestly? I was a little thrown when you said you were going to hang with him, but I actually think it's pretty cool that you and he can still be friends."

"Really?" Elizabeth blurted.

Jeff chuckled. "Yeah," he said. "I mean, I'm not Mr. Enlightened. I can't say I wouldn't feel better if the guy had a hump and a harelip . . . and maybe some really bad acne. . . ."

Elizabeth laughed and shook her head, digging into her lunch. How had she lucked out and gotten a second chance with Jeff French? And why was she thinking about jeopardizing it?

"So anyway, what do you want to do this weekend?" Jeff asked, just before sucking a long strand of spaghetti into his mouth.

"I don't know," Elizabeth answered. *Just nothing*

on Friday because I'm seeing the guy you're so not paranoid about again. "Maybe we can do something on Saturday?"

"Saturday's good," Jeff said with a nod. "Why don't we go see that new movie? You know, that mushy romantic comedy you've been hinting about for the past two weeks."

"You caught that, huh?" she asked. She had to admit, the guy was good.

"You've only mentioned it a hundred times. And left my mom's magazine open to the ad on the living-room table last week," Jeff shot back with a smile. "How could I miss it?"

If you were Conner, you would have, Elizabeth thought. *He never picked up on anything.*

She looked into Jeff's kind green eyes and tried to smile while swallowing back the ever-present guilt. Jeff was so . . . perfect. While Conner was so . . .

Infuriating, Elizabeth thought.

She looked up and caught a glimpse of Conner skulking across the cafeteria in his battered suede jacket, and her heart caught in her chest. Why did he make her feel that way when she knew firsthand what a disaster he was as a boyfriend?

"You okay?" Jeff asked, leaning over the table a bit.

"Yeah, I'm fine," Elizabeth said, taking a bite of

her salad. "Sorry. I just spaced for a second. I'd love to see the movie on Saturday night."

"Great," Jeff said. "Maybe we can grab something to eat beforehand. We could try that new place we didn't get to go to the other day."

"I'm in," Elizabeth said. Then she looked down at her plate and pretended to concentrate on eating.

She couldn't consume much, though, considering what a panic attack her insides were having. She'd be spending Friday with Conner and Saturday with Jeff. How had she gotten herself into such a mess?

Just tell Jeff you're seeing Conner again, Elizabeth told herself, glancing at her boyfriend. *He doesn't seem to mind, so why don't you want to tell him?*

Elizabeth shifted in her seat, trying to calm the nervousness in her stomach. She didn't want to tell Jeff because seeing Conner didn't feel as innocent to her as it seemed to be to him. And she was worried that if she told him, he would see that fact written all over her face.

Maybe after Friday I'll be less confused, Elizabeth thought hopefully. She glanced at Conner, who was now sitting at Elizabeth's regular table with Tia, Andy, Maria, Ken, and Jessica. Her sister was telling a story and had everyone's rapt attention, but Conner, of course, was focused on a magazine he had laid out in front of him on the table. Elizabeth smiled. Vintage Conner.

Then, as if he felt her watching, Conner lifted his eyes and looked right at her. Startled, Elizabeth glanced away, her heart pounding. This was insane. No matter how great she knew Jeff was, her reactions to Conner only seemed to be getting more intense.

Suddenly Jeff reached over, picked up Elizabeth's free hand, and kissed it. Elizabeth smiled but felt a little foreboding thump of guilt.

Maybe by Saturday I'll be letting Jeff down easy, she thought.

"So . . . Cherie," Melissa said, hooking her arm around her friend's shoulders as they headed for the water fountain during a break from practice. The rest of the squad trailed behind them, chatting and laughing. "You haven't mentioned the big birthday date with Aaron."

Cherie looked down at the ground and shrugged, and Melissa pulled her arm away. "There's not much to tell, really," Cherie said, reaching up to tighten her curly red ponytail. "Let's just say Aaron is kind of hard to read."

Funny. I can read him just fine, Melissa thought, forcing herself not to smirk.

"What do you mean?" she asked, leaning up

against the wall as Cherie bent over the water fountain. She took a long drink, then wiped her mouth with the back of her hand and stepped aside so Melissa could take a turn.

"Well, I know *I* had a good time," Cherie said, letting out a sigh. "And Aaron seemed to have fun too. I mean, he *said* he did. But I'm pretty sure he didn't like his gift."

Melissa stood up straight and shot Cherie a concerned look. "Did he say he didn't like it?" she asked, moving aside so Jessica could get at the water fountain.

"No. He said it was great," Cherie said. "But he said it all flat, you know? Like the way you respond when your grandmother gives you socks. 'Oh . . . this is . . . great,'" she said tonelessly, her face a picture of boredom.

"Ah," Melissa said with a knowing nod. "Well, don't worry about it. Gifts are tough."

"True," Cheri said, crossing her arms over her stomach as she started to shuffle back toward the lobby, where the team was practicing. "But I was hoping . . . I don't know . . . I guess I was hoping a good gift would give me an in, you know? Now I have no idea what it's going to take to get this guy's attention."

Melissa smiled to herself, looking down at her

sneakers and letting her hair tumble in front of her face so that Cherie wouldn't notice. It was really almost too easy.

"Don't take this the wrong way," she said slowly. "But what if you started to dress a bit more . . ." She trailed off to make herself sound hesitant—polite.

"A bit more what?" Cherie asked, stopping in her tracks. It was clear from her voice that she was on the verge of being offended.

"Well, you *are* kind of a tomboy," Melissa pointed out gently. She gave Cherie an apologetic little frown and looked over her clothes—a beat-up, faded Seattle Seahawks T-shirt and a pair of guy's gym shorts.

"I'm dressed for practice," Cherie said, looking down.

"Yeah, but . . ." Melissa glanced in the direction of the rest of the squad, all of whom were wearing slim tank tops or sport halters and cute shorts. Cherie followed her gaze and flushed slightly.

"So . . . what? You think Aaron likes a girly-girl?" Cherie said, raising her eyebrows skeptically. "I don't know if I like the idea of changing the way I dress for a guy. Doesn't that go against the whole liking-me-for-me thing?"

"No! Not at all!" Melissa said, starting to walk again. "It's not like you dress like a slob or something. All it would take is some very minor changes. You know, a skirt here and there."

"I don't really own many skirts," Cherie said, biting her bottom lip.

"So? You'll borrow some of mine," Melissa said with a shrug. "You can come over after practice. It'll be fun."

Cherie paused in front of the lobby and looked away, obviously thinking the plan over. Melissa could tell she was torn about changing her image, but Melissa had a feeling that Cherie's crush on Aaron would win out in the end.

"All right," Cherie said finally.

Yes! Melissa thought.

"Thanks for the offer," Cherie added as they walked into the lobby. "You've been really great about all this."

"Anytime," Melissa said happily.

By the time Jeremy walked into Rafferty's with Stan after basketball practice on Thursday, he was so hungry, he felt like he was going to collapse before he got a chance to order. Ever since he'd gotten his weekend sickness out of his system, he'd needed to eat almost nonstop.

"Two deluxe burgers and Cokes," he said to the lady behind the counter. "And we're gonna take 'em in the back."

"You got it, hon," the woman answered. Then she

shot him a disturbed look when he grabbed a handful of peppermints out of the bowl next to the register.

"Bad breath," Stan whispered in excuse.

The guys cracked up laughing as they headed to the back of the restaurant toward the pool room. The El Carro transfers had turned them on to this hangout at the beginning of the year, and Jeremy was pretty much addicted to their burgers. He and Trent used to come here at least twice a week to chow down and shoot some pool. Of course, that ritual had ended a long time ago.

"Thanks for coming with me," Jeremy said to Stan as he slipped out of his varsity jacket and hung it on one of the hooks on the wall. He popped one of the mints into his mouth and took a deep breath as his stomach grumbled loudly. "I don't think I could have taken another tense dinner at the Maynors'."

"No problem, my friend," Stan said, grabbing a pool cue off the wall. "But I gotta tell ya, we're all starting to wonder when you and Trent are gonna start talking again already."

Jeremy felt his face flush at the thought of all his friends talking about the stalemate between him and Trent. "I don't know," he said. "Let's just play."

Stan seemed to take the hint and started to rack up the balls. "Now, you know I suck at this, right?" he warned Jeremy.

"You can't be that bad," Jeremy said, chuckling as he chalked up his cue.

"Oh, you'd be surprised," Stan said. He leaned his hulking frame over the table, wielding his cue awkwardly, and attempted to break the balls. The cue bounced back in Stan's direction and the rest of the balls moved about a millimeter each.

Jeremy hung his head.

"Told ya," Stan said happily.

As Jeremy took his shot, smacking the balls in all directions and sinking a couple of solids, he couldn't help remembering what those ritual visits with Trent were like. They'd play wild games of nine ball, betting their PlayStation cartridges against pizzas and CDs. Their games would get so intense, people would actually stop what they were doing to watch and place their own bets on the outcome.

Stan took another shot and sank one of Jeremy's balls and the cue. Clearly this game wasn't going to be quite like that.

"Sorry," Stan said, shrugging his large shoulders.

"You'll catch on," Jeremy said.

But when he lined up to take his next shot, he felt an unmistakable pang of nostalgia. What was he doing? Trent should be here right now. Maybe he was taking this whole thing too far. Maybe all he was doing by refusing to forgive was cheating himself out of a best friend.

Stan walked around the table, looking for a good shot, and Jeremy took the opportunity to think back to everything that had happened between him, Trent, and Jessica. And still, even now, he felt his face redden with anger when he thought about how Trent had betrayed him. He couldn't foresee any possible situation in which he'd be able to forgive Trent.

Okay, if I keep thinking about this, I'm going to ruin my night, Jeremy thought, gripping his cue.

He pushed himself away from the wall, took his shot, and decided to concentrate on teaching Stan how to play pool.

As Elizabeth leaned back in the passenger seat of Conner's black Mustang on Friday afternoon, she couldn't help but feel that she was doing something forbidden. And it made her smile.

She looked over at Conner, who was, of course, concentrating on the road, and felt like it was September all over again. When she and Conner had first met, first been forced to live together, first started to date. These rides in the car used to be the most exciting *and* excruciating few moments of her day as she wondered what Conner would say to her.

Elizabeth hadn't realized how much she'd missed feeling like this. Feeling psyched and nauseous at the same time.

Conner reached down to shift the car into fourth, and his pinky brushed her knee just below the hem of her skirt. Elizabeth froze as a jolt of tingling electricity shot throughout her entire body. He yanked his hand away as if her skin had burned it and slapped it back onto the steering wheel. Heart racing, Elizabeth glanced at him out of the corner of her eye. His lips were pressed together as if he was trying to keep from screaming.

Okay, okay, okay, Elizabeth's brain said over and over. *Everything's fine.* Her hands were pressed into the seat at either side of her, and they were so sweaty, she was sure they were leaving stains on the vinyl seat cover. She picked them up and leaned her elbow against the door, trying for a casual posture. Instead she just felt completely awkward and conspicuous.

"Uh . . . thanks for driving," Elizabeth said, feeling the need to break the intense silence. "Jessica had to go right to work after school."

"Yeah," Conner said. "No problem."

She couldn't help but notice that his fingers gripped the steering wheel a bit tighter. He had to be feeling the tension in the car as well. It was all Elizabeth could do to keep from grinning as he turned the car onto his block and she glimpsed his house up ahead.

Were they really going to spend the afternoon studying? Maybe it would start out that way, but they couldn't ignore the almost palpable . . . sizzle in the air between them, could they? Elizabeth wrapped the shoulder strap of her bag around and around her hand, wondering where he would suggest they work once they got there. If he suggested the kitchen, that would mean he wanted to keep things platonic. But if he mentioned his room or even the den . . .

Elizabeth bit her lip as Conner pulled the car into the driveway. She held her breath as he cut the engine. They both sat there for a moment in perfect silence.

"So," Conner said, his hands still on the wheel. Then he looked at her, and Elizabeth felt the intensity of his gaze all the way down to her toes. "Ready?" he said.

Elizabeth's throat was completely dry. "Yeah," she answered.

Ready as I'll ever be.

Jeff French

She's thinking about getting back together with him. I'm not saying she's going to, but she's thinking about it.

I know I played it cool this afternoon, but I'm not an idiot. I can tell when someone I care about is feeling conflicted. She couldn't keep her eyes off of him again all through lunch. I should have just called her on it. Why didn't I? I'm such a wuss. But I know why I didn't. Because I didn't want to hear the answer. Even if she lied. <u>Especially</u> if she lied.

Because I don't think I could handle it if Elizabeth dumped me for her ex . . . <u>again.</u>

I just have to hope that she won't.

Because I think I'm still in love with her.

Elizabeth sat back into the cushy couch in Conner's den and tried to focus her attention on her notes. Any second now she was going to get around to revising this story. She was. If she could just get her heart to stop pounding and somehow make her eyes quit glancing over at Conner.

Was he inching closer to her, or was it just her imagination? No. She was sure he'd started out at the other end of the couch, and now he was definitely closer to the middle. She knew it! She knew he'd picked the den for a reason.

"I think I'm going to revise the guitar story," Conner said suddenly, causing Elizabeth's heart to slam against her rib cage.

"Oh, yeah?" Elizabeth said, clutching her pen so hard, it almost slipped out of her sweaty grasp. "What about the new assignment?"

"I know, I just can't stop thinking about the other one," Conner said, glaring down at his notebook. "If

I don't revise it now, I'm not going to be able to concentrate on anything else."

Elizabeth nodded and looked down at her notes again, but she didn't see a single word. Maybe Conner wanted to talk the story over with her because he wanted to try to find a way to tell her that it was actually *about* her. Her pulse picked up the pace a bit, and she tried not to grin. Maybe he wanted to change the ending . . . make it so that the musician was actually reunited with his beloved guitar in the end.

Elizabeth screwed up all her courage and turned to face Conner, pulling her legs up onto the couch and crossing them Indian style. "Well, what do you think needs to be done?" she asked. She yanked the afghan off the back of the couch and covered her legs with it, then rested her notebook on top of her lap.

"It needs more . . . action," Conner said, squinting. He pushed his hands into his hair and held it back from his face for a moment, then let it flop forward again. "I think the musician needs to destroy the guitar."

Elizabeth felt like the world had dropped out from under her. He couldn't be serious. "Destroy it?"

"Yeah," Conner said, squirming back in his seat and leaning over his notebook. He was obviously excited by his new idea. "I could have a scene where he, you know, smashes it into the stage or something. Shards flying everywhere."

Swallowing hard, Elizabeth looked down at the multicolored afghan. "You paint a good visual," she said. This couldn't actually be happening, could it? He wanted to *smash* the guitar? What was he trying to say with *that*? "But . . . don't you think it goes against the theme of the story?" she said hopefully. "I mean, it's really poignant when he goes looking for it in the end. He can't exactly do that if he knows he destroyed it."

"Yeah, I'm thinking about changing the ending too," Conner said. "Too sappy."

"Oh . . . right. Of course," Elizabeth said flatly. She could feel all the blood slowly draining out of her face as doubt started to seep in. It was nearly impossible for her to admit it, but she was starting to think she might have been wrong about the true meaning of Conner's story.

Unless he was trying to tell her that he wanted her dead. In which case, she was really *hoping* she'd attached false meaning to his story.

"What do you think?" Conner asked, looking at her for the first time. His green eyes were gleaming with excitement.

Elizabeth opened her mouth hesitantly and

looked down at her notebook. "I . . . I think that if that's where you want the story to go, then you should change it," she said, her heart so heavy, it was sagging close to her stomach.

"Are you okay?" he asked bluntly. "You look a little . . . off."

Well, I'm a complete and total idiot . . . and I'm evil . . . but other than that I'm fine, Elizabeth thought.

"No, I'm okay," she said, flipping to a clean page in her notebook. "I just . . . I have a lot to do."

Conner seemed to accept this, and he went back to slashing up his story with his pen while Elizabeth concentrated on not crying.

I'm such a moron, she thought. How could she have ever let herself believe that Conner wanted her again? Worse than that, how could she have ever believed that *she* wanted *Conner* again? They'd been nothing but trauma for each other when they were together, and now that she and Jeff—

Jeff, Elizabeth thought, her heart twisting when she thought of his open, honest face. *What would he think if he knew where I was right now?*

She sighed and leaned back again, creative writing suddenly the last thing on her mind. She was going to have to find a way to make the last week up to Jeff. If that was even possible.

* * *

"Thanks for driving me around today, Aaron," Melissa said, pulling her hair back in a ponytail to keep the wind from whipping it around.

Aaron's idea of a car was a Jeep Wrangler with no top, no doors, and a couple of surfboards where the backseat should have been. It was more like riding in a dune buggy than a car, but Melissa was enjoying it, especially after another afternoon of successful tutoring/flirting.

"It's no problem," Aaron told her, downshifting as he sped around a corner. Melissa grabbed the roll bar and laughed. "You've been sacrificing your afternoons to help me. The least I could do is help you out when your car's in the shop," he added.

Melissa looked at him through her cat-eye sunglasses. "Trust me, the last few days have not been a sacrifice," she said, with just a hint of flirtation.

Aaron glanced at her, one eyebrow raised, as if he was trying to figure out if he'd heard her right.

Yeah, you did, Melissa thought, looking through the windshield again. *I am flirting.*

And her car wasn't in the shop. She'd just made that up so that Aaron would have to drive her to his house after school and home after tutoring. A little extra time to execute her plan.

"So, how are things with Cherie?" Melissa asked nonchalantly.

"There isn't really a *thing* with Cherie," Aaron said, lifting one shoulder. Melissa's heart actually warmed when he said this. He didn't seem interested in the girl at all.

I am just too good, Melissa thought with a smile.

"I don't know, she's nice and everything, but I'm really not sure she's my type," Aaron continued, his hair whipping around his forehead in the wind. "I thought she was, but I don't know."

"Okay, explain," Melissa said, even though she knew exactly what he meant. She wanted to hear the guy say it.

"Well, I mean, I know this is going to sound weird, but did you see that dress she wore today?" Aaron asked, taking his eyes off the road for a second to look at her.

"Yeah . . . ," Melissa said. It was hers, after all.

"Well, I don't know, one of the things I liked about her in the first place was that she was so laid-back. I kind of have a weakness for tomboys," he said with a sexy smirk.

"Oh," Melissa said, looking down at the zip-front sweatshirt she was wearing over a baby T. As if she didn't know that little tidbit.

Aaron turned onto Melissa's street, and she sighed, almost not wanting to go home. She'd really had fun with Aaron that afternoon. Plus she'd love to hear more about how very *not* right Cherie was for him.

"Besides, Cherie and I don't seem to mesh, you know?" Aaron said suddenly, as if he'd read her thoughts and was granting her wish. "We obviously don't have the same taste in music, and I doubt she'd go for my taste in movies."

He pulled into Melissa's driveway and slammed on the brakes, lurching them both forward.

"Sorry," he said. "Bad habit."

"No problem," Melissa said, trying not to wince from the pain where her seat belt had cut into her chest. She unbuckled it and turned to look at Aaron. "So, what makes you think Cherie doesn't like classic movies?" she asked.

A slow grin spread across Aaron's face, and he laid his arm on top of the steering wheel. "Well, I figure I can't be lucky enough to meet two girls who appreciate the classics in one week."

Melissa let out a flirty little giggle, and as she did, she managed to work in a subtle snort. She covered her mouth and nose with her hand and looked over at Aaron, as if she was embarrassed, but Aaron was just looking at her with total disbelief and unmistakable attraction.

"I can't believe I just did that," Melissa said, blushing.

"No, don't worry about it," Aaron said, his deep blue eyes looking into hers. "It's kind of cute."

Melissa's heart gave a little extra thump, and her blush deepened. But she wrote it off as normal. Her pulse tended to quicken whenever a cute guy flirted with her. And Aaron was *definitely* cute. She just sat there for a moment, looking back at him, and she was sure he was thinking about kissing her. Finally he blinked and sat up straight, clearing his throat. He'd obviously just remembered that she was attached to Will.

Still, it was a fact that was apparently shrinking in importance to Aaron. Melissa's plan was working. She could feel it.

Friday night, Trent sat on the opposite end of a bench in the locker room from Jeremy, feeling a lot more than the normal game-night tension. He pulled his jersey on over his head and glanced at his former friend, whose back was turned to him. This was truly unbelievable. They were supposed to be teammates. Trent had dealt with Jeremy's cold shoulder through enough games. This had to stop.

He shoved his feet into his sneakers and tied them extra tight, planning out what he was going to say.

Don't be confrontational, he told himself. *Just say good luck or something. Give him an opening. He has to come around sometime.*

A couple of the guys jogged past him, shouting and laughing and getting themselves riled up for the game. Trent took a deep breath and let it out slowly, then stood and squared his shoulders. Jeremy was just standing up and slamming his locker. It was now or never.

"Hey, man," he said, coming up behind Jeremy, whose shoulders visibly tensed. Not the best sign. "I just wanted to say good luck tonight."

Jeremy turned around slowly, his jaw set and his eyes as cold as ice. He just stared at Trent for a second as if he wanted him to disappear.

"Yeah, good luck," he said coldly. Then he brushed past Trent and headed out to the gym.

Suddenly Trent was filled with a burning anger he had never felt before in his life. His fists clenched at his sides, and his eyes narrowed as he turned around to watch Jeremy storm through the locker-room door. Part of him wanted to call Jeremy back and just settle this thing right now, but he didn't, and the opportunity passed.

"Not now," he told himself. "Just chill, man."

He couldn't make a scene. Not when they were about to play a game. Not only would their coach freak out, but if a fight ensued, which, considering the fact that he couldn't seem to unclench his hands was bound to happen, they'd probably both be benched. And if he and Jeremy were both benched, they'd definitely lose the game. All because of something that *didn't* happen a while ago.

Trent took a deep breath and tried to clear his head. He'd talk to Jeremy later. For now, at least he could use this anger in the game.

Alanna Feldman was living her worst nightmare. The Boy Toy concert was even worse than she'd imagined. There were girls from the ages of four to twenty-four, screaming and clutching signs and crying all around her. The music was awful. The dancing, worse. And she couldn't understand what the whole attraction was anyway. The only time she'd even cracked a smile was when the chunky member of the group had misstepped and fallen on his face, taking a microphone and amp with him.

Finally . . . *finally* . . . the last encore song drew to a close, and Alanna grabbed her mother's wrist. "It's over. Let's go," she said, wanting to get out before the crowds filled the aisles.

"Don't you want to see if they—"

"No, thanks," Alanna said. She practically dragged her mother up to the stadium's concourse just as all the lights went on, signaling that the torture was, in fact, over.

"Omigod! Alanna *Feldman?*"

Alanna glanced up, all the color draining from her face as Laura Seager, Jenny Moskowitz, and Marci Reynolds came running up to her. There weren't three girls at her school that Alanna detested more. And the loathing was only solidified by the fact that they each had the words *Boy Toy* written across their faces in blue lettering.

"I never thought I'd see *you* at one of *these,*" Marci said, crossing her arms over the front of her tight Boy Toy T-shirt and eyeing Alanna skeptically.

"Yeah, well, wonders never cease," Alanna said, sidestepping them. She walked so fast, her mother could barely keep up, but she hardly cared. All she could think about was the fact that by Monday, everyone at school would know that she had attended the big Boy Toy concert . . . with her mother. Maybe she could plead temporary insanity.

"Alanna! What is the rush?" her mother asked when they reached their car a few minutes later. She was out of breath and looked more than a little perturbed. Alanna started pulling at the door handle well before it had been unlocked. "You'd think you didn't even want to be here!" her mother added, sounding shocked and disappointed.

Suddenly all the anger and discomfort Alanna had been feeling all week came bubbling to the surface and she exploded, right there in the middle of the parking lot.

"I *don't* want to be here!" Alanna shouted, holding her hands out at her sides. "I would rather be back in *rehab* than be here right now."

"Alanna!" her mother hissed, looking around as a few mothers hurried their daughters along.

"No one cares, Mom!" Alanna shouted. "But all *you* care about is what *they* think! This entire week all you've been doing is buying me presents and doing all this stupid, girly, silly stuff with me. I don't want presents! I do not wear pink! And I *hate* Boy Toy!"

A pack of girls walking to their car stopped to gasp at her last comment, but Alanna just rolled her eyes. She walked around the car and stood in front of her stunned mother.

"All I want is a mother who actually *listens* to me," she said, embarrassed as she choked on the last few words.

Then Alanna saw something she was sure she'd never seen before. Her mother started crying. Hard. It was totally silent, but there were definitely tears streaming down her face.

Suddenly Alanna's heart felt like it was breaking.

"Oh, Mom, don't . . . don't do that," she said, reaching toward her mother. It felt awkward, though, and she drew her hands back uncertainly.

"I'm so sorry," her mother said through her tears. "I just . . . I feel so stupid. I don't even know how to talk to my own daughter."

"It's okay," Alanna said, finally reaching out and hugging her mother. "Really, Mom, it'll be fine."

Her mother wrapped her arms around her and hugged her back in a way that she never had before. Alanna smiled as her mother continued to cry. Now they were getting somewhere. She'd never felt this close to her mother in her entire life. It was weird, but it was a nice weird.

"I just wish you could trust me like you trust your friends," her mother said, pulling back and touching Alanna's cheek with her palm. "Or Conner," she added.

Alanna felt her face redden and was about to tell her mother that she was wrong—that she couldn't trust Conner—but something stopped her. She just looked into her mom's tearful eyes for a moment and realized that she was actually hugging her mother. That she was standing here in a parking lot and she was actually having an emotional connection with her mom.

And it was all because of Conner.

If he'd never brought her parents to Chicago. If he'd never cared enough to try to bring them together, they definitely wouldn't be here now. Conner actually *was* trying to help her.

"Mom?" she said. "I need to see Conner."

Her mother opened her mouth, and for a split second Alanna was sure she was going to criticize Conner. But she seemed to think better of it. She sniffled and pulled a tissue out of her purse. "Okay, honey," she said miserably.

"No! Not because I don't want to talk to you," Alanna said, hoping her mother wouldn't think she was trying to ruin the moment. "I just . . . I haven't talked to him in a while and . . . it's hard to explain, but I *really* need to talk to him."

"I understand," her mother said with a small smile. "I'll take you home so you can get your car."

"Thanks, Mom," Alanna said with a grin.

She ran back over to her side of the car and climbed in, feeling an intense mix of relief and nervousness. She had no idea what she was going to say to Conner when she saw him, but suddenly she couldn't wait to say whatever it was.

"That band really was awful, huh?" her mother said as she started the car.

Alanna laughed. "Mom, I think there's actually hope for you."

Jeremy Aames

I want to forgive Trent. I really do. I mean, I miss my best friend, as lame as that sounds.

But every time the guy tries to talk to me, I get all tense. This anger just, like, takes over and I can't even see straight. And I always end up saying something that makes me sound like a complete jerk.

I hate it. But I can't seem to control it.

Why can't I just get past this?

CHAPTER 10

A Killer Play

"I can't believe we're actually doing this," Elizabeth said to Conner with a small smile.

"I know," he answered quietly. He looked deeply into her eyes and smirked. "Give up?"

"Never," Elizabeth shot back.

She looked down at the Scrabble tiles in front of her and studied the board. Okay, so the night hadn't turned into some kind of romantic kissing fest, but this wasn't so bad. After they'd decided they couldn't take working anymore, they'd decided to whip out the old game. She really never thought she'd see the day that she and Conner would be hanging out and having fun together again.

"Ah!" she said suddenly, actually causing the ever placid Conner to flinch. She picked up her letters and slapped them down on the board in front of her. "Earwax," she said triumphantly. "And the *x* is on a triple-letter score! Ha!"

"Liz, *earwax* is two words," Conner said.

"No, it's not. It's one," she protested.

"It's two," Conner said, crossing his arms over his chest. "Wanna bet?"

"Are you challenging?" Elizabeth said, leaning back in her chair and arching one eyebrow. She tilted her head and smiled at him tauntingly. "Because you know that if you challenge and you're wrong, you lose a turn."

Conner rolled his eyes. "You are such a goody-goody," he said, his green eyes flashing.

"Why? Because I follow the rules?" she asked. "Oh! I forgot! Conner McDermott isn't a play-by-the-rules kind of guy," she added sarcastically. "Excuse me. I forgot I was in the presence of the King of Cool himself."

In one swift motion Conner reached into his soda glass, pulled out an ice cube, and flung it at Elizabeth. She ducked, but it still hit her shoulder and fell in her lap. Elizabeth shrieked, picked it up, and flung it back but missed and knocked half the letters off the Scrabble board.

"Nice one," Conner said. "Do that because you knew you were losing?"

Elizabeth's face heated up. "You are so dead," she said with a laugh. She picked up her water glass and lurched around the table to dump it over his head, but he grabbed her wrist and stopped her, throwing his other arm around her back and holding her so she couldn't move.

"Let go!" Elizabeth shouted, struggling through her laughter.

"Not until you give up the glass," Conner said, laughing himself.

"Not gonna happen," Elizabeth said.

And so they just stood there, arms outstretched with his hand locked around her wrist, neither of them giving an inch.

"Um . . . Conner? We're going to have to move sometime," Elizabeth said, turning her face toward his. When she did, her mouth was right next to his neck, and the scent of his aftershave overtook her, sending a shiver through her body.

Was it ever going to be normal to be close to him?

Conner turned his head slightly so that their faces were only inches apart. He gazed at her for a moment, and she knew. In that moment she *knew* he could feel it too. Whether the guitar story was about her or not. Whether he wanted to get back together with her or not. Whether he loved Alanna or not, he was still attracted to her.

"On the count of three," he said huskily. In that moment Elizabeth wasn't sure if they were going to part or kiss when he got to three.

"'Kay," she said.

"One . . . two . . . three."

He let go of her and stepped away, and the sizzle in the air disappeared. Feeling let down, confused, and suddenly exhausted, Elizabeth put the water glass down on the table and let out a silent sigh. Conner stood a few feet away from her, hands in the back pockets of his jeans, looking at her like he wasn't quite sure what she was doing there.

Then the doorbell rang.

"Who the hell?" Conner turned and walked out of the room, leaving Elizabeth frozen in place.

Taking a deep breath and shaking her head in an attempt to clear the confused fog, Elizabeth started to pick up the scattered Scrabble tiles. Then she heard Tia's voice coming from the foyer and smiled. It would be so nice to have someone else here to break the bizarre tension. She dropped everything and walked out of the kitchen to say hello, but her face fell the moment she saw the girl at the door. It wasn't Tia. It was Alanna.

And Elizabeth's reaction was nothing compared to hers. The moment she laid eyes on Elizabeth, she appeared to lose all the color in her face. She glanced at Conner, her eyes questioning and accusing at the same time, then turned and ran. Elizabeth's stomach dropped so quickly, she almost got dizzy. She couldn't imagine what Alanna was thinking at that moment, but she knew it wasn't good.

Conner turned his head slowly to look at Elizabeth, but she couldn't read his expression. And before she could apologize to him, he took off after Alanna, leaving Elizabeth entirely alone.

Trying to get control of his breathing, Trent bent at the waist and braced his hands above his knees, waiting for the Palisades forward to inbound the ball. It had been a rough game so far, and Big Mesa had taken a serious beating in the first half. But now, thanks to some creative playing by Trent and his teammates, they were catching up, slowly but surely. Trent stood up straight as the ball reentered the court and focused on covering his man.

They had to win this game. If not, this day was going to go down as one of the worst of his high-school life.

The Palisades forward dribbled up the court, then tried to pass to his teammate, but Chris Robinson got there first and whacked the ball toward Trent. As soon as the ball hit his fingertips, Trent was on the move, blowing past the stunned Palisades players on the way to the net. There was no one near him. A perfect opportunity for a killer play.

Knowing this was the shot that would tie the

game, Trent bit his lip, launched himself into the air, and jammed the ball through the hoop. It was unnecessary showmanship, but the crowd went wild. And Trent felt good for the first time all day.

Until he came back down to the ground.

The moment Trent's feet hit the floor again, he felt a sharp pain in his right leg. He let out a shout as he doubled over and fell to the floor, smacking his right side against the hard wood. He clutched his knee to his body, writhing around in pain. Whistles blew, spectators groaned, and sneakers came squeaking to a stop, but Trent didn't hear any of it. All he could hear was his mind repeating over and over: *This is not good. This is not good. This is not good.*

"Maynor! Maynor, are you all right?" His coach's voice broke through the stream of consciousness.

Trent tried to straighten his leg, but the pain was excruciating, and he pulled it up again. Sweat poured down his forehead and into his eyes, and he scrunched up his face in agony.

"Maynor?"

"Just give me a sec, Coach," he said through his teeth. He locked his jaw and tried again, and somehow he moved through the pain. Once his leg was straight, the pain wasn't as bad, and he blinked up at the people that had gathered around him. The trainer, the coach, Chris, and Jeremy.

Like you really care, Trent thought out of nowhere.

"You all right?" asked John Stacito, the team's trainer, putting out his hand.

Trent clasped John's arm, and together they managed to hoist him off the ground. The crowd applauded as Trent limped around, testing his leg. It definitely hurt, but it seemed like it was functioning.

"I'm fine," he said as John came over with arms outstretched to help him walk around. "I'm fine. Let's play."

He looked at the coach, who blew out a sigh of relief. "Good," he said. "Let's go, ref!"

Trent limped back to the center of the court, wondering if he looked as banged up as he felt. If he did, he definitely wasn't going to be intimidating his opponents. He tried to stand with all his weight on both legs, but a bolt of pain prevented it. Instead he leaned most of his weight to his left while trying to look like his right foot was touching the ground.

Come on. You can do this, he told himself. *It's just a little injury.*

Moments later the game started up again, but when Trent tried to hog down court, his leg almost gave out on him. Pain shot up his leg and radiated throughout his body, but he sucked it up and kept playing. He couldn't let his team down. Not after fighting back from such a deficit.

But the first time he got the ball, when he tried to take it to the basket, he was running at about one-third his usual speed. Trent gritted his teeth as he dribbled, but the pain was too distracting. One of the Palisades players knocked the ball out of his hand fairly easily and scored.

"Time!" Jeremy yelled, throwing his hands up to form a T.

Trent put his hands on his hips and glared at Jeremy. He wasn't really wasting a time-out to ream him over one botched play, was he? The team convened by the bench, Trent bringing up the rear, and Coach asked Jeremy what was up.

"I think we should take Trent out, Coach," Jeremy said, without so much as a glance in Trent's direction. "In fact, I think he needs to go to the hospital."

"What? Are you kidding me?" Trent exploded.

"I'm sorry, but your leg is obviously killing you," Jeremy said, turning his head to look at him. "If you keep playing, you could really damage it."

Trent shook his head, leveling Jeremy with a glare. He couldn't believe the guy was actually taking his stupid grudge this far. Did he really want to lose an important game over it? "This is unbelievable, man. Like you really care about my leg."

"Trent—"

151

"No, man! I'm sick of this!" Trent shouted. "How many times am I supposed to apologize? I'm sorry, all right? I'm sorry I made a play for your girl. But if this is how you're gonna deal with it, man, you got issues I don't even wanna touch!"

The entire gymnasium fell silent for a split second, and all the hairs on the back of Trent's neck stood on end. Had everyone really just heard that?

Jeremy sighed. "Coach?" he said, obviously choosing to ignore everything Trent had just said. "It's your call."

Trent's heart fell the moment Coach turned to face him. He could tell by the man's expression that he was agreeing with Jeremy. Trent's face burned with fury and embarrassment. Jeremy couldn't do this to him. Not now that everyone was watching and knew what was really going on.

"I have to agree with him, Trent," Coach said, rubbing the back of his neck. "I'd rather lose you for one game than for the rest of the season."

"Fine!" Trent shouted, limping over to the bench. He sat down hard, trying not to wince from the incredible pain he felt. He glared at the floor, unable to look at the crowd or at anybody else in the room. Trent had never been so humiliated in his entire life.

The next time he got Jeremy alone, he was going to make him admit that he'd taken him out of the game for personal reasons. Whatever it took, he was going to make him admit it.

Melissa moved to the driving dance beat that was blaring through the speakers at the Sweet Valley gym, dancing in perfect time with the rest of the squad. They were coming to the end of their half-time routine, and she was living it up. There wasn't much Melissa enjoyed more than a gym full of people watching her every move.

A formation change required that she turn to face the back of the gym, and just as she did, the basketball team started filing back out to the sidelines from the locker room. She scanned their faces until she caught a glimpse of Aaron. Like all the other guys, he was watching the squad and trying to look like he wasn't.

Boys, Melissa thought with a smirk as she turned around again, still dancing. *They want us to think that they're too focused on the game to notice us. Please!*

The dance ended, and Melissa did her standard jump-up-and-down-and-shout thing that she did at the end of every cheer. As she did, she made a point to turn around again, and this time Aaron was blatantly watching her. Not the squad. Not Cherie. But her.

The second she caught his eye, Aaron blushed a deep red and looked away, pretending to be totally engrossed in whatever his coach was saying. Melissa grinned, feeling elated. She couldn't believe it! He was really checking her out!

She glanced over her shoulder as the squad returned to the stands, and Aaron was looking at her again. This time he didn't look away, and the sheer boldness of his stare made Melissa's heart skip a beat. She blushed and smiled back, her gaze locked with Aaron's. It was like she couldn't look away.

"Melissa!" Tia called from the sideline. "We're changing the quarter cheer!"

Snapping out of whatever bizarre trance she was in, Melissa joined the rest of the squad as Tia explained what she wanted to do between the third and fourth quarter. She barely registered the instructions, though. She was too busy wondering what had just happened. The moment she'd just shared with Aaron was twenty times more intense than the little flattery-induced blush she'd experienced the day before.

Melissa took a deep breath and tried to focus. What was going on with her?

*   *   *

"Alanna!" Conner shouted as she tore across his lawn and whipped open the driver's-side door of her car. His heart felt like it was being ripped right out of his chest. The look on her face when she'd seen Elizabeth standing there . . . he didn't even want to think about it. This was like sick déjà vu—that time when Alanna came back from rehab and found him kissing Elizabeth in his kitchen all over again. Except that back then, he'd truly been torn between the two girls. Now he knew exactly who he wanted—but he had no clue how to make her believe him.

He jogged toward her car, hoping she'd relent and let him explain, but she peeled out moments before he got there and took off down the street, tires screeching the whole way.

His heart pounding, Conner looked at his car— felt the keys jabbing into his leg through his front pocket. He could just get in and take off after her, but he hesitated. Did he really want to be *that* guy? The pathetic guy that chases his ex-girlfriend down all because of a misunderstanding? She was the one who had totally blown him off. She was the one who had refused to talk to him for days. Was it really any of her business if he had Elizabeth over on a Friday night?

Unfortunately, the only answer that came to mind was, *Yes.*

Before he could overthink it, Conner jumped into the Mustang and tore out of the driveway. There were a lot of lights between his house and hers. Chances were he would catch up to her at one of them.

He took a turn way too fast and saw Alanna's car up ahead. He gunned the engine and the car lurched forward, cutting off some guy who was trying to get into his lane.

"Sorry, buddy," Conner muttered under his breath, his hands gripping the steering wheel. He was behind Alanna now but a few car lengths back. He wasn't sure if she'd noticed him yet, and he hoped she hadn't. If she did, there was a good chance that she was just crazy enough to try to lose him.

They were coming up to a light, and Conner glared at it, willing it to turn yellow. Magically it did, and Alanna stopped—the first car at the stoplight. Conner pulled up behind her, put his car in park, opened the door, and started to climb out, but the second he did, he caught Alanna's eye in the side mirror.

She looked at him and narrowed her eyes, and then her face hardened with resolve.

"Don't!" Conner shouted the moment he realized what she was about to do.

Alanna slammed on the gas and squealed through the red light and the four-way intersection, nearly getting slammed by a rental truck. Shakily Conner dropped back into his seat and closed his door again. He slumped back, his mouth dry with fear, his heart slamming away in his chest, and stared at the traffic whizzing by his windshield in front of him. He couldn't believe she'd just done that. She'd actually almost gotten herself killed just to get away from him.

What was he supposed to do now?

Alanna Feldman

You know, people have always told me that dreams do come true. And now I know they're right.

Because I just lived my worst nightmare.

Never Looking Back

Elizabeth came home to a dark, empty house on Friday night—a perfect match for her gloomy mood. She trudged through the living room and right into the kitchen, hoping a little cookie-dough ice-cream therapy would do the trick, even though she knew in the back of her mind that sugar wasn't the answer.

In one night she'd gone through the whole range of emotions—excitement, hope, total letdown, guilt, guilt, and more guilt. And then, of course, she'd had to endure the ride home from Conner. After he'd gotten back from not finding Alanna, he'd driven her all the way back to her house managing not to utter a word or look at her even once.

There was no way ice cream was going to solve this one.

But it's worth a try, Elizabeth thought, pulling the fresh pint out of the freezer. She grabbed a spoon, slammed the cutlery drawer with her hip, and was about to head for the den and some mindless TV when she noticed the light on the answering machine was blinking.

She scooped out a heaping spoonful of ice cream and hit the play button just before stuffing her mouth. The machine let out a loud beep, and then the message started.

"Hey, Liz, it's Jeff. . . ."

Elizabeth's heart twisted the moment she heard his voice. His sweet, happy voice. She leaned against the wall, feeling like the last of her energy was draining right out of her.

"I just wanted to tell you I'm looking forward to tomorrow night. I know this sounds lame, but it's like I miss you or something, which, of course, doesn't make sense since I just saw you this afternoon, but—" He laughed, and Elizabeth could practically see him shaking his head at himself. "Anyway, I'll talk to you later and . . . sorry to anyone else who may have had the misfortune of hearing this message." Another laugh. "Bye."

Elizabeth sighed, staring at the machine as it rewound. "I am a huge jerk," she said matter-of-factly. "There is no instrument in the world capable of measuring what a tremendous jerk I am."

She grabbed her backpack off the chair where she'd tossed it and climbed the stairs to her room, awkwardly spooning ice cream from the carton along the way. The moment she flicked on the light in her bedroom, her eyes fell on the bulletin board above her desk. Right smack in the middle was a picture of her and Jeff that had been taken at the beach the weekend before.

Elizabeth dropped her bag and walked over to the board, leaning in close to study the photo. She had climbed up on Jeff's back, piggyback style, and when the picture had been taken, she was about to slide off. They were both laughing, and Elizabeth couldn't help thinking she never looked that happy in any of the pictures she'd ever had taken with Conner.

She dropped the pint of ice cream on her desk and pulled her photo album out of the bottom drawer, quickly flipping open to the middle, where she knew there were a few shots of her with Conner. Sure enough, not one of them was as bright and happy as the picture on her board. She was smiling, but there was no light in her eyes. And Conner never smiled in pictures. Any casual observer would have thought he was miserable to be with her.

"I bet he doesn't look like this in any pictures with Alanna," Elizabeth muttered to herself, thinking of the way Conner had taken off after his ex that evening. It was almost romantic. At least, it would have been if it hadn't been her ex-boyfriend chasing after his true love.

Elizabeth dropped the album back into the drawer and slammed it. Enough was enough. It was clear that Conner didn't want her back. And if she thought about it—if she really forced herself to think about it—it was possible that all the excitement she'd felt over the past week had been in her head. She was still attracted to Conner, yes. But she knew they were completely wrong for each other. She knew he'd make her miserable if they got together.

Lowering herself onto her bed, Elizabeth did something she'd been avoiding for the past few days—she made herself think things through. And when she did, she realized that she didn't love Conner anymore. In fact, she wondered if she ever had. It was quite possible that back when she and Conner had gotten together, she'd mistaken intense attraction and a massive crush for love.

But with Jeff, it's different, she thought, standing again. She pulled the picture off the bulletin board, and her pulse started to race when she looked at it. Jeff was kind, and he understood her, and he cared about her, and he was a good person. He made her feel special, which was more than she could say for Conner the Stone-faced.

"That's it," Elizabeth said, tossing the picture onto her desk. She grabbed the ice cream and headed downstairs to put it away. After that, she was outta here. She was going to go over to Jeff's house and plant a big old kiss right on his lips.

And once that was done, she was never going to look back.

How did I end up here? Trent asked himself, staring down at his bandaged leg, which was propped up on a chair in front of him. The doctor was snapping x rays up on a light board that hung on the wall behind his desk, explaining the position of his hairline fracture. His parents sat on either side of him, leaning forward with rapt attention as the doctor spoke, but Trent couldn't seem to tune in to what the guy was saying. He was too busy seething about Jeremy.

He still couldn't believe that Jeremy had insisted on coming along to the hospital. It wasn't like he actually *cared* what happened to Trent. As captain of the basketball team, it was clear that the guy just wanted to make sure he didn't lose his best player. Either that or he was hoping for a good gloating opportunity. If it turned out that Trent had a serious injury, Jeremy's taking him out of the game was going to be justified. And Trent was sure Jeremy

163

would like nothing more than to be able to say, "I told you so."

"Well, Trent, it's a good thing your parents brought you in here," Dr. Jacoby said, coming around his desk and leaning back against it. "If you'd kept walking on that leg, you would have done some real damage. And I don't even want to think about what would have happened if you'd continued playing tonight."

Trent's face burned. This guy was saying practically the exact same thing Jeremy had said earlier. It was really too bad Jeremy was out in the waiting room right now. He would have loved to hear this.

Humiliated, Trent slumped even lower in his chair. He expected his leg to respond with a stabbing pain at the movement, just like it had every time he'd so much as flinched since the injury had happened, but he felt nothing. Apparently the painkillers were doing their job.

But they couldn't, of course, keep him from feeling like a complete idiot. Apparently Jeremy *had* done him a huge favor by taking him out of the game tonight. Which meant he'd not only made an idiot of himself by announcing to half the school that he'd tried to steal Jeremy's girlfriend, but he'd been wrong about Jeremy's motivations as well.

"You'd definitely be sitting the rest of the season out, that's for sure," Jacoby continued with a smile. He scratched at the top of his balding head and pulled Trent's chart off his desk. "As it is, you should be back within six weeks," he said, studying the papers.

"That's great," Trent's father said with a relieved sigh. His parents both looked at him, obviously expecting him to respond.

"Yeah, it's great news," Trent said, barely lifting his eyes. And it was. Of course, it also meant that Jeremy was definitely never going to talk to him again. Not after the way he'd treated him tonight. Not now that he was right and Trent was wrong—*again*.

This day just kept getting better and better.

"What is taking so long?" Jeremy muttered, lacing his fingers together and squeezing his hands as he sat in the hospital waiting room. Words couldn't express how badly he hated this place. Jeremy had spent way too much time in Fowler Memorial Hospital with his father this year. And once his parents had moved to Arizona with his sisters, he hadn't expected to be back here anytime soon.

Yet here he was, heart pounding, sweat glands working, worried out of his mind once again. He didn't know what he would do if Trent was really hurt. He did know that if Trent was out for the season, the guy would be devastated. He loved basketball. And Jeremy's heart actually ached with sympathy at the thought that that might be taken away from his best friend.

Best friend, he thought, slumping back in his highly uncomfortable chair. *Is that what he is?*

Jeremy leaned his head against the wall and stared up at the porous ceiling. It was time to let it go. Trent *was* his best friend. And sitting here freaking out about his future had brought that fact home to Jeremy in crystal-clear relief. Trent had been there for him through everything that had happened this year. He'd even given Jeremy a place to stay when his parents had been forced to move because of his father's deteriorating health.

Maybe Jeremy couldn't forget that Trent had tried to get with Jessica, but he couldn't forget all of the great things Trent had done for him either. Yeah. It was definitely time to let it go.

The door to the exam rooms flew open, and Jeremy looked up. Trent was maneuvering his way through the swinging doors slowly . . . on a pair of crutches.

Oh, no, Jeremy thought. He stood up, clutching his jacket in one hand. His shoulders tensed as he waited for Trent and his parents to cross the ER.

"What is it?" Jeremy asked when Trent stopped in front of him. "Are you okay?"

"Yeah. I'm fine," Trent said through his teeth.

"We'll go get the car, honey," Mrs. Maynor said, touching Trent's shoulder. "You should try to sit and relax for a minute."

Trent looked down at the gleaming floor as his parents disappeared through the automatic sliding doors. Jeremy could practically feel the tension in the air, but he had no idea what to say. Things did not look good.

Shifting awkwardly, Trent started to turn himself around so that his back was to the chairs.

"Need help?" Jeremy asked.

"I said I'm fine," Trent snapped. He fell into a chair and groaned, then dropped his crutches to the floor with a clatter.

Jeremy swallowed hard, watching his friend try to find a comfortable position. He knew it wasn't going to be easy to make up with the guy, and he had no idea where to start.

"It's just a hairline fracture," Trent said, glancing up at Jeremy, his expression hard. "But I guess I should thank you. If you hadn't taken me off the court when you did, I'd be in a lot worse shape."

A wave of relief rushed through Jeremy, and he

167

blew out a sigh. He was about to tell Trent how happy he was for him, but Trent quickly looked away. It was clear that he was hurt, and not just in his leg. And it wasn't like Jeremy could blame him.

"Look, man, I'm sorry for being such a moron for the last few weeks," Jeremy said finally, shifting his weight from one foot to the other. Trent blinked but didn't move. "I mean it, Trent. I'm sorry."

After a few moments of tense silence that Jeremy thought would never end, Trent finally glanced up at him. He seemed to realize that Jeremy was sincere because his expression finally softened.

"Yeah?" Trent said. "So . . . we're cool?"

Jeremy smirked. "Yeah, I mean, I think that little performance you put on in the gym tonight was punishment enough," he joked, sitting down next to him.

Trent blushed furiously, but he looked at Jeremy, laughter in his eyes. "So you mean all this time all I had to do was publicly humiliate myself?" he said. "Man, why didn't you say so?"

They both laughed, and Jeremy felt his heart lighten for the first time in weeks. Finally, after all this time of being angry and tense, it was actually over.

Elizabeth was so nervous when she rang Jeff's doorbell, she felt like she was picking him up for their first date. The moment she heard his bounding footsteps approaching the door, she realized she hadn't even bothered to look in a mirror, and she frantically ran her fingers through her hair, pressed her lips together, and pinched her cheeks.

"Liz!" Jeff said, his whole face lighting up the moment he opened the door. Elizabeth's heart responded with a huge thump, and she grinned right back. Then she reached up, wrapped her arms around his neck, and stood on her toes to kiss him before he could say another word.

Clearly stunned, Jeff took a moment to respond, but then he pulled her close to him and deepened the kiss, sending chills up and down Elizabeth's spine.

"Surprise," she said softly as they parted.

"A good one," Jeff said, not remotely loosening his grip on her waist. "Where'd you come from?"

"Nowhere interesting," Elizabeth said with a smile.

"Well, it's nice to see you," Jeff said, pulling her inside and slamming the door with his foot. "I don't know if you got my insane message, but—"

"I did," Elizabeth said with a smile. "And I missed you this week too."

It wasn't a complete lie. When she'd been focused on Conner, she had realized that she was being completely stupid. She had realized what she was doing to Jeff. And she felt so relieved to be in his arms now, she couldn't believe she'd lived without it all week.

"I'm sorry I've been so spacey lately," Elizabeth said, taking a step away from him. She looked him in the eye. "But I'm back now. That's all over."

Jeff took a deep breath and reached out to hold both her hands. "It is?" he asked seriously. "You're sure?"

Elizabeth's brow creased as she looked back at him. It was as if he knew what had been going on. Like he was asking her if she was really over Conner. But that was impossible. She was obviously just being paranoid.

"I'm sure," she answered breezily, squeezing his hands. "So . . . can I make it up to you?"

"What're you thinking?" Jeff asked with a grin.

"How about . . . a nice long night of cuddling in front of the TV?" Elizabeth suggested.

Jeff leaned forward and kissed her forehead. "I'm in," he said.

As they walked hand in hand to the living room, Elizabeth couldn't stop smiling. She was so lucky to have Jeff, and she was so glad she hadn't let herself make a huge mistake with Conner. How could she have even considered giving up a perfect guy for one whose only skill was breaking her heart?

WILL SIMMONS
12:05 A.M.

I think something's wrong with Melissa. She went back to the locker room to change for the postgame party tonight, and when she came out, she was wearing jeans, sneakers, a sweatshirt, and almost no makeup.

I don't know much about mental illness, but is it possible she's having an aneurysm or something?

CONNER MCDERMOTT
12:16 A.M.

I can't sleep. I can't stop thinking about Alanna. I want to go over there and explain. And I want to find out what she was doing here. But I can't make myself get up.

Because what if she's not there? If she never went home and then I showed up at her house, her parents would definitely freak. They'd think she ran away again, and they'd blame me. And that's something I do not want to deal with.

Not again.

TIA RAMIREZ

12:19 A.M.

I'M NOT CRAZY. THERE WAS DEFINITELY SOMETHING WEIRD WITH CONNER AND ELIZABETH THIS WEEK. AND AS MESSED UP AS THAT WHOLE RELATIONSHIP WAS, AT LEAST CONNER WAS <u>CONNER</u> WHEN HE WAS WITH LIZ.

I'VE NEVER LIKED ALANNA. I'VE TRIED, REALLY. AND IT'S NOT THAT I DON'T WANT CONNER TO BE WITH HER IF SHE MAKES HIM HAPPY. BUT SHE DOESN'T. YEAH, HE SEEMS TO THINK SHE DOES, BUT FROM WHAT I'VE SEEN, ALL SHE DOES IS TURN HIS LIFE INSIDE OUT.

UNFORTUNATELY, I DON'T THINK CONNER'S CLOSE TO OVER HER.

SO WHATEVER THIS NEW THING
WAS WITH ELIZABETH, I HAVE A
FEELING I'LL STILL BE LISTENING
TO HIM DRONE ON ABOUT
ALANNA.

FOR NOW, AT LEAST.

MELISSA FOX

12:22 A.M.

I had such a perfect time at the party tonight. Will was so obviously baffled by what I was wearing, but that's another story. I ended up spending a lot of time with Aaron, actually. The three of us were hanging out—me, Will, and Aaron—and then a bunch of guys wanted to play volleyball out back. Will went, but Aaron stayed with me. Will even told him to take care of his girl. Ha!

So we were sitting on this love seat in the fairly packed living room, talking about <u>Rear Window</u>, when Cherie walked in. She looked <u>so</u> uncomfortable in my clothes. But the moment she saw us, her face lit up. She must have thought I was talking her up to Aaron. So she came over and sat down with us, and about ten seconds later Aaron made some lame excuse to leave.

It was so funny! Cherie was so devastated, I almost felt bad for her.

Almost.

ELIZABETH WAKEFIELD
12:30 A.M.

I had such an amazing time with Jeff tonight. Just lying around watching TV with him is totally romantic. Especially when he gives up trying to pay attention to the dumb plots and starts kissing my neck and my ear and my . . .

Well, let's just say I'm so glad I got over that whole bout with Conner insanity.

I wonder if he ever talked to Alanna tonight.

Check out the **all-new**....

(Sweet Valley Web site—)

www.sweetvalley.com

New Features

Cool Prizes

The **ONLY** official Web site!

Hot Links

(And much more!)

BFYR 202